'You can't help yourself. You want me,' Dante said in a deep, thickened voice.

'No, I hate you,' Beth said hoarsely.

His face was like carved granite, his eyes hard. Suddenly he moved and a long arm shot around her. His large hand splayed across her back whilst the other grasped the back of her head and jerked her body towards him. He dipped his head, his mouth crashing down on hers, relentlessly prising her lips apart to the powerful thrust of his tongue.

Shocked and furious, she tried to pull away, but his hands clamped her in position. Her head was so close she could not drag it from beneath his all-consuming mouth. While the steel band of his arm holding her pressed her hard against his long body she tried to struggle, but he was too strong, and shamefully, instead of feeling revulsion, she was floundering in the wave of heady sensation flowing through her body.

Her voice seemed to have deserted her, and her heart was thudding so hard she thought it might burst. Her passionate hatred of him was overtaken by a passionate desire.

Jacqueline Baird began writing as a hobby, when her family objected to the smell of her oil painting, and immediately became hooked on the romantic genre. She loves travelling, and worked her way around the world from Europe to the Americas and Australia, returning to marry her teenage sweetheart. She lives in Ponteland, Northumbria, the county of her birth, and has two teenage sons. She enjoys playing badminton, and spends most weekends with husband, Jim, sailing their Gp.14 around Derwent Reservoir.

Recent titles by the same author:

RETURN OF THE MORALIS WIFE
PICTURE OF INNOCENCE
THE SABBIDES SECRET BABY

**Did you know these are also available as eBooks?
Visit www.millsandboon.co.uk**

THE COST OF
HER INNOCENCE

BY
JACQUELINE BAIRD

MILLS
BOON

First published in Great Britain 2013
by Mills & Boon, an imprint of Harlequin (UK) Limited.
Harlequin (UK) Limited, Eton House, 18-24 Paradise Road,
Richmond, Surrey TW9 1SR

© Jacqueline Baird 2013

ISBN: 978 0 263 23446 6

Harlequin (UK) policy is to use papers that are natural, renewable and recyclable products and made from wood grown in sustainable forests. The logging and manufacturing process conform to the legal environmental regulations of the country of origin.

Printed and bound in Great Britain
by CPI Antony Rowe, Chippenham, Wiltshire

THE COST OF
HER INNOCENCE

PROLOGUE

'I REPEAT, MISS MASON, do you understand the charge brought against you by this court?'

Jane, in a voice choked with fear, finally answered, 'Yes.'

She still could not quite believe she was standing in the dock, accused of being in possession of a Class A drug with intent to sell. She was in her second year of a Business Studies course and worked five evenings a week in a fast food café to help pay her way through college. This whole thing was like a nightmare and she hoped she would wake up at any second....

But it was no nightmare. This was reality, she finally accepted as the curt tone of the judge's voice demanded, 'How do you plead? Guilty or not guilty?'

She gripped the handrail of the dock to steady her trembling body and, lifting her head, cried, 'Not guilty!'

Why would no one believe her? She glanced desperately across at Miss Sims, the lawyer the court had appointed to defend her, but her attention was on the notes in her hand, not Jane.

Dante Cannavaro lounged in his chair while the preliminaries were adhered to. The case was not one he would normally consider, but Henry Bewick, the head of the law firm where Dante had worked as an intern at the beginning of his career, had asked him to assist as a personal favour to him.

At twenty-nine, Dante was now an international lawyer, specialising in commercial litigation. He had not acted in a criminal trial in years, but he had read the case, and as far as he could see it was cut and dried.

A car had sideswiped Miss Mason's. When the police officer attending the accident had asked to see her driving licence the girl had fumbled around in her tote bag and a suspicious-looking package had fallen out, which had proved to be full of drugs. The only passenger in her car had been a rather drunk Timothy Bewick—son of Henry. The girl had denied all knowledge of the drugs. Her defence was that someone else— she'd implied Henry Bewick's son—must have put the drugs in her bag.

Dante had met Timothy Bewick, and it was obvious the boy was besotted by the girl and reluctant to give evidence against her. Dante, having seen a photograph of Miss Mason, could understood why. A tall, black-haired beauty, in a skimpy top and shorts that displayed her generously curved body and long legs to perfection, Miss Mason was enough to tempt any man. A testosterone raging teenager stood no chance. Dante had agreed to take the case.

He raised his head as she adamantly declared herself not guilty. *Liar,* he thought, studying her with his dark assessing eyes. Today she had played down her looks, wearing her hair scraped back into a tight knot at the back of her head, no make-up and a black suit—probably at her lawyer's suggestion.

But in fact Miss Sims had done her client no favours. From Dante's point of view Miss Mason had played right into his hands. The severe tailoring of her suit fitted her firm breasts, narrow waist and round hips perfectly, and made her appear older than her nineteen years—which would help his case when he called Timothy Bewick to the stand. When the jury compared the two it would be obvious who was telling the truth—the young, lovestruck boy.

He stood up and smiled cynically, deliberately holding her gaze. He saw her big eyes widen pleadingly and thought he witnessed a gleam of sensual awareness in their depths. He noted the flick of her tongue across her lush lips and wasn't fooled for a moment—though surprisingly he felt a sudden tug of lust. God, she was good. No wonder young Bewick was crazy about her! Dante remembered all too well how that felt! Yes, he had definitely made the right decision… It would give him great pleasure to take the delectable Miss Mason apart in the dock and he proceeded to do so.

Jane looked at the tall, black-haired man who stood up to face her. He smiled at her and her breath caught in her throat. Her tummy churned and her heart leapt with hope. At last a friendly face! From his perfectly chiselled features to his long, lean, solidly built body he radiated confidence, concern and pure masculine power. *This* man would recognise she was telling the truth. She knew it instinctively….

How wrong she had been, Jane realised bitterly as the prison gates clanged shut behind her. Numb with fear, she looked up at the forbidding building that would be her home for the next three years—or, if she was lucky, half that time with good behavior, according to Miss Sims, her worse-than-useless lawyer....

'I hate to leave you here, Helen,' Jane said, looking at the older woman with tears in her eyes. 'I don't know how I would have survived without you these past eighteen months.' She hugged the friend who had literally saved her life.

'Thank you for that,' Helen said, kissing her cheek and stepping back with a smile on her face. But her expression grew serious. 'Now, no more tears, Jane. Today you are a free woman. Stick to the arrangements we have made and you will be fine.'

'Are you sure I can't visit, Helen? I will miss seeing you terribly.'

'Yes, I am sure. My daughter lost her life at eighteen, and a lousy lawyer and so-called friends almost ruined yours. Remember what I told you: the world isn't fair, so never dwell on the injustice of the past—that will only consume you with bitterness. Think only of your future. Now, go—and never look back. Clive Hampton, my lawyer, will be waiting for you and you can trust him. Listen to him, and be careful, confident and proud of the successful woman I know you will become....' She gave her a hug. 'Good luck.'

CHAPTER ONE

'GOODNIGHT, MARY,' Beth Lazenby called to the receptionist as she walked out of the offices of Steel and White, the accountancy firm in the centre of London where she was a junior partner. She paused for a moment on the pavement and took a deep breath, glad to be out in the fresh air—or not-so-fresh air she thought ruefully. She enjoyed her work, but just lately, and especially when she spent time at the cottage, she questioned whether she really wanted to spend the rest of her life in the city.

Beth watched the people hurrying past her, their day's work finished. It was rush hour, and when she saw the length of the queue at her usual bus stop she decided to walk to the next one. The exercise would do her good, and apart from Binkie she had nothing to hurry home for. Her friend Helen had died three years ago from cancer—four months after she had been released from prison on parole.

Dismissing the sad memory, Beth looped her bag over one shoulder and walked on. A tall, striking woman, with red hair that gleamed like fire in the evening sun, her slenderly curved body moved sinuously beneath the grey linen dress she wore as she strolled along. But Beth was oblivious to the appreciative glances of every passing male. Men did not figure large in her life. She had a successful career and was proud of what she had achieved. She was content.

Suddenly she saw a man a head taller than most of the crowd walking towards her and she almost stumbled. Her heart started to race and she swiftly averted her gaze from the black-haired man she hated with a vengeance. A man whose dark satanic image was engraved on her mind for all time—the lawyer Cannavaro, the devil himself as far as she was concerned, and he was a mere ten feet away.

She heard Helen's voice in her head. *Be careful, confident and proud of the successful woman I know you will become.*

Beth tilted her chin at a determined angle and carried on walking. At least Helen had lived long enough to see her success, and she would not let her down now. Cannavaro would never recognise her. The naive Jane Mason was gone for ever, and Beth Lazenby was nobody's fool. But the hairs on the back of her neck stood on end as she passed him, and out of the corner of her eye she caught the look he gave her. Did he hesitate? She didn't know and didn't care. She simply kept on walking. But her sense of well-being faded as memories of the past flooded her mind. Her full lips tightened bitterly as she wondered how many more innocent victims the vile Cannavaro had sent to prison in the past eight years.

She recalled the naive teenager she had been, standing in the dock, frightened out of her wits. Cannavaro had smiled at her, and the deep, sympathetic tone of his voice when he'd told her not to be nervous or afraid had given her hope. He'd said he and everyone else present only wanted to discover the real truth of the case…. Stupidly, she had believed him. He had been her knight in shining armour, her saviour. But then Timothy Bewick and his friend James Hudson had both lied on the stand, and by the time she'd realised her mistake it was too late—she'd been found guilty. Her last view of Cannavaro as she'd been led from the court had been of him and her lawyer talking and laughing together as if she didn't exist.

Dante Cannavaro was feeling good. He had just won a deal for his client—a multinational company—for substantially more money than they had expected. Dismissing his waiting driver, he'd decided to walk to his apartment, where the customised Ferrari he had ordered was due to be delivered in an hour. A satisfied smile curved his lips.

Striding along the pavement he found his dark eyes caught by the flaming red hair of a beautiful woman walking towards him and he lingered, the car suddenly forgotten. She was tall—about five-nine, he guessed—and wearing a conservative grey dress that ended an inch or so above her knees. The dress would have looked bland on most females, but on her it looked stunning, and his captivated gaze roamed over her slender but shapely body and long legs in primitive male appreciation.

He paused, his head automatically turning as she passed him. The gentle sway of her hips was enough to give a weaker man a coronary. In Dante's case it was not a hardening of the arteries in the heart that troubled him, but the hardening of a different part, much lower down. It wasn't surprising he had such a reaction to her, he thought. She was beautiful and sexy and he had been celibate for a month, he reasoned. Before reminding himself that he was engaged to Ellen.

As an international lawyer, Dante had offices in London, New York and Rome. He kept an apartment in all three cities, but considered his real home to be the estate in Tuscany where he'd been born, which had been in his family for generations.

Dante's Uncle Aldo—his father's younger brother and head of Cannavaro Associates in Rome—had died last March, and it had been pointed out to him at the funeral that *he* was now the last remaining male Cannavaro. It was time he stopped indulging his preference for international law, concentrated on the long-established family firm and settled down and had a son or two—before the Cannavaro name died out completely.

Dante had assumed he would marry and have children some day, but now, at the age of thirty-seven, he had suddenly been made to face his duty. He wanted children, hopefully a male heir, while he was still fit enough to be an active father. And so he had chosen Ellen, because he had known and respected her in a professional capacity for a couple of years and she ticked all the boxes. She was intelligent, attractive, and she liked children—plus, as a lawyer, she understood the demands of his work. And the sex between them was fine. It was a perfect partnership, and once Dante made a decision he never changed his mind. Other women were off the agenda for good.

But the redhead was a stunner, and it was in the male psyche to *look*…he consoled himself.

An hour later Beth smiled as she walked down the Edwardian-style terraced street. Unlocking the door of her one-bedroom ground-floor apartment, she entered the hall and kicked off her shoes, slipping her feet into a pair of slippers. She grinned as the only male in her life strolled over and rubbed against her ankle.

'Hi, Binkie.' She bent down and picked up the ginger cat and nuzzled his neck. She walked down the hall, past her bedroom, the living room and the bathroom, to the rear of the building, and entered the largest room— the kitchen-diner.

She put Binkie down, switched on the kettle and opened the cupboard, taking out a can of cat food.

'You must be starving,' she said, filling his bowl with the tuna flavour he loved before placing it on the floor. In seconds his head was in it. With a wry smile at the foolishness of talking to her cat, she made a cup of coffee and, taking a sip, crossed to the back door that was set in the side wall of the kitchen. Opening it, she stepped out onto the patio.

The garden was Beth's pride and joy, and the flowers she had planted in a few tubs on the patio were a blaze of colour. Strolling past them, she admired her handiwork with a sense of satisfaction, and then walked on to the lawn that was framed by a four-feet-high brick wall, with a gate opening into the garden of the two-bedroom apartment above her.

On the other side of her garden a high trellis had been fixed to the wall, and was completely covered by scented jasmine intertwined with clematis. She took another sip of coffee and looked around her with pleasure, dismissing the sighting of Cannavaro from her mind. He wasn't worth a second thought. She walked back to the patio and sat down on one of the wooden chairs that circled the matching table to drink her coffee and admire her handiwork in peace.

But just as she began to relax Beth's neighbour, Tony, appeared, leaning on the gate. Tony was sturdily built, with short fair hair and a round, cheeky face and had just turned twenty-three. Beth felt a lot more than four years older than him and his flatmate, Mike. The boys worked at the same City bank, and were a pair of fun-loving young men without a care in the world.

'Hi, Beth. I've been waiting for you to get home. Mind if I join you?'

Not waiting for an answer, Tony strolled through the gate.

'What is it this time? Sugar, milk or are you begging a meal?' she asked dryly, watching as he straddled a chair and propped his elbows on the back.

'For once, none of the above.' He grinned. 'But I wouldn't mind sex, if you're offering,' he declared with a mock-salacious grin.

Beth couldn't help it. She laughed and shook her head. 'Not in a million years, Tony Hetherington.'

'I thought not. But you can't blame a guy for trying,' he said, his blue eyes sparkling with humour. 'But, to get down to business, are you at home this weekend or are you going to the cottage again?'

'No, I'll be here for the next two weeks and then I'm taking three weeks' holiday to go down and do some much-needed decorating—and with luck get in some surfing. I'm hoping you'll keep a check on this place, as usual. You do still have the spare key?'

'Yes, of course. Consider it done. But to get back to my problem... As you know, Monday was my birthday and I had dinner with my parents—boring! So on

Saturday I plan to have a party for all my friends, and *you* are invited! We're a bit short on women, so please say you'll come.'

'Why am I not flattered by the invite?' Beth queried mockingly. 'Making up the numbers is bad enough, but I also remember your last party, at Christmas, when I served most of the food and drink and then ended up chasing the guests out when you and Mike passed out! Not to mention cleaning up afterwards....'

Tony chuckled. 'That was unfortunate. But it was a great party—and it will be different this time, I promise. For a start, it's going to be a barbecue. The guests are invited for four in the afternoon until late, and we'll be outside, so no cleaning up.'

'Ah! I see. So what you really mean is can you use my garden as it is twice the length of yours?'

'Well, there is that, yes—but more importantly Mike is making a list of the food he thinks we need. Personally, I think a few dozen sausages and burgers and a bit of salad would do, but you know what he's like— he thinks he's a great cook. He's talking marinated chicken, special kebabs, fish and stuffed heaven knows what! As for the salads—you name it and he is going make it. You *have* to help me, Beth,' he declared, looking at her with pleading puppy-dog eyes.

'You are *such* an actor,' she said dryly. 'But your boyish charm does not wash with me.'

'I know, but it was worth a go.' He grinned. 'But, honestly, I really do need your help. We had a barbecue last month, when you were away for the weekend, and it was a bit of a disaster,' he confessed sheepishly. 'I knew you wouldn't mind, but unfortunately Mike nearly poisoned half the guests with his stuffed pork loins. We will never hear the end of it from our pals at the bank.'

'Oh, my God, he didn't?' Beth exclaimed with a laugh.

'Oh, yes, he did,' Tony said wryly, getting to his feet. 'Which, when I think about it, is probably why we are short on females this time. What right minded girl is going to risk getting food poisoning again?'

'All right, all right. I'll come and help,' Beth agreed when she could stop laughing. 'On condition the barbecue is set up in *your* garden. I don't want any of my plants burnt—which is quite likely to happen with you two in charge. The guests can use my garden to drink, eat…whatever. But my apartment is strictly out of bounds. Understood?'

'Yes, you gorgeous woman, you. We can keep the beer bins on your patio.' He grinned and walked back though the open gate. 'And thanks!' he called back, before disappearing into his own apartment.

At seven on Saturday evening the sun was shining in a clear blue sky, and a relaxed smile curved Beth's lips as she looked around the garden, which was crowded with casually dressed people. Some were eating, drinking or standing chatting, whilst others were already dancing to the music. A few more guests were upstairs in the boys' apartment, where the hard liquor was being served. Beer and white wine was stacked in big bins full of ice outside Beth's kitchen window. She had taken the precaution of locking her back door, and had the key in the pocket of her jeans.

'Alone, Beth?' A slightly inebriated Tony slid an arm around her waist. 'That will never do. Thanks to you talking Mike out of his flights of fancy over the food, the barbecue is going great and the party is really taking off. Have a drink.'

Smiling, she shook her head. 'You know I never drink.'

'Well, I'm going to get another—catch you later.' Tony's arm fell from her waist and he half turned, then stopped. 'I don't believe it!' he exclaimed, grabbing her waist again. 'My big brother is here! I left a message at his London office, inviting him, but I never expected him to come. He's a lawyer—the intense, intellectual type—and he speaks about six languages and travels all over the world with his work. In fact he's a workaholic. I haven't seen him since last year, but Mum told me he finally got engaged a couple of months ago. I guess the woman with him must be his fiancée.'

'I didn't know you had a brother,' Beth said with a curious glance past Tony. Then she froze.

There in front of her she saw a hard, handsome face with heavy-lidded eyes that seemed to look straight at her, before the man turned to smile down at the woman by his side. Fear gripped Beth for a moment at the sight of the couple Mike had just led into the garden, and he was now indicating where she stood with Tony.

Cannavaro. It could not be! She stared in disbelief at the tall, broad-shouldered man walking towards them and felt a shiver run down her spine.

Beth noted that the thick black hair was longer now, and brushed the white collar of his shirt. Belted chinos clung to his lean hips and followed the long length of his legs. She stiffened as an icy coldness washed over her. There was no mistake—it was him....

She had only ever seen Cannavaro in a dark suit—the

man in black who had haunted her dreams, her night-mares, for years. But he was just as intimidating in casual clothes, if not more so. His relaxed appearance would fool anyone into thinking he was one of the good guys. Not the smooth-talking devious devil Beth knew him to be.

Beth had not set eyes on him since her court appearance eight years ago. She had followed Helen's plan and with the help and guidance of Clive Hampton had settled in London, where it was easy to go unnoticed among the teeming millions of people. Or so she had thought until now.

The odds against bumping into Cannavaro even once in London must be huge, but twice in a week they'd be astronomical... Or just sheer bad luck. And she was going to have to deal with the situation coolly and con-fidently. Running away would simply draw attention to herself.

But surely Cannavaro could not be Tony's brother? For starters he was a lot taller, and he looked nothing like him. Tony was fresh-faced, young, fun, and he laughed his way through life. Cannavaro had black hair, olive-toned skin and, though handsome, his face held a hard ruthlessness, an arrogance that she recognised all too well. Secondly, and more importantly, they had different surnames.

'You don't look anything like each other,' she probed cautiously.

'Same mother. Different fathers. I take after my dad. Mum's Italian, and she was a widow with a thirteen-year-old son when Dad met her in Italy. They married almost immediately and he brought her back to England to live. Dante went to school and university in Italy and

England, so we only saw each other on the holidays—
half of which we used to spend at Mum's old home in
Italy. Mum and Dad still go there, but I haven't been
for years. Being stuck in the middle of the countryside
is not my idea of fun, but Dante loves the place. Actually, it belongs to him now, as he inherited his father's
estate and oodles of money along with half of the family law firm.'

It was that simple. They actually were brothers! Beth
was horrified, and her whole body tensed. She was appalled at the thought of being in the hateful man's presence for even a minute, let alone all evening.

She listened with a sinking heart as Tony continued
speaking. 'With a fourteen-year age difference between
us I've always been a bit in awe of him. Dante has it
all—tall, good-looking, fit and incredibly wealthy. He
doesn't need to work so hard or even at all. I keep telling him, but he just ignores me. He's far too cerebral for
my mind, but he is a great guy when you get to know
him, and all the women adore him. I'll introduce you.'

'No,' Beth said abruptly. 'You and your brother must
have a lot to catch up on, and I need to feed Binkie.'

She tried to excuse herself but Tony's hand tightened
on her waist when she tried to move.

'The cat can wait. Do me a favour, Beth, and play
along with me. With a stunner like you on my arm,
for once I will get one over on my big brother. He has
played the field discreetly for years with a string of
beautiful women. To be honest I'm surprised he's decided to get married…. His fiancée looks lovely, but
she's not as nice as you.'

Beth didn't get a chance to refuse….

'Good to see you, Tony,' a deep, dark voice drawled,

and Beth froze in Tony's hold at the hauntingly familiar sound of the man's voice.

'And you, Dante. I'm surprised you could make it.' Tony grinned and shook his brother's hand. 'And this must be the fiancée Mum told me about.' Tony smiled at the woman at his brother's side.

Dante Cannavaro smoothly made the introductions. 'Ellen, this is my younger brother, Tony.'

'Lovely to meet the woman who can tame Dante,' Tony declared with a grin and, dropping his arm from Beth's waist, he introduced her to the other woman.

Beth shook hands with Ellen and almost felt sorry for her as they exchanged the conventional greetings. She looked to be in her early thirties, her hair perfectly styled, her face perfectly made-up, and her casual trousers and top both designer label. She smiled, but there was condescension in the smile as her blue eyes took in Beth's department-store apparel. Some of Beth's sympathy for the woman faded.

'Congratulations on your engagement. I wish you both a very long and happy marriage,' Beth lied through her teeth. Personally, she hoped Cannavaro's life was hell. 'Have you chosen your dress yet?' she asked enthusiastically. She was not in the least interested, but it delayed the moment when she would have to face the man she despised, and gave her time to control her wildly beating heart and the shock of seeing him again.

Cannavaro was the man responsible for sending Beth to prison, and she had nearly died the first week she had been there. A group of women had thought that because she was in prison on a drugs charge she had the contacts to supply them with drugs. When she had told them she was innocent and that she had no knowledge of drugs she had been dragged into the showers and stripped. Her hair had been cut off and she'd been told her throat would be next... Luckily Helen, a middle-aged woman and her cellmate of three days, had walked in and saved her.

It had been Helen who had convinced her to change her name to Beth Lazenby when she was released, and had made it possible for her to do so. Ironically, the women who had cut off her hair had helped too. Beth was naturally a redhead, but as a child she had been teased unmercifully from her first day at school, and as she had grown taller and bigger than most of her class the bullying had gotten worse.

Finally, when she had been fourteen and they had just moved from Bedford to Bristol for her father's work, her mother had suggested that Beth dye her hair dark before she attended a new school and made new friends. Beth had quickly agreed and the bullying had stopped. Her life had been content for a number of years—until she had turned eighteen and had been in her first year at college.

Her parents, on their first holiday without her, had tragically died when the cruise liner they were on had sunk off the coast of Italy. This had been heartbreaking for Jane as the parents she had lost had been her adoptive parents, who had taken her in when she had been just a baby. Jane had no idea who her biological parents were, and had suddenly found herself all alone in the world.

So the day Jane Mason had walked out of jail after serving eighteen months of her sentence she'd been almost unrecognisable. Her hair had returned to its natural red colour and she'd been almost two stone lighter in weight. With Clive's help she had legally changed her name by deed poll to Beth Lazenby.

Helen's plan for Jane to change her name had made perfect sense; it was hard enough for an innocent young woman to make her way in the world without the totally unjustified tag of a prison sentence on her CV.

Beth owed it to the memory of her friend to show no weakness now.

CHAPTER TWO

DANTE CANNAVARO WAS not in a good mood. When he had called at Ellen's apartment earlier, contemplating their reunion after a month apart, he had casually mentioned his brother's barbecue and suggested they call in. Ellen had yet to meet Tony, and Dante was considering asking him to be his best man at their wedding. Ellen had hated both ideas. Barbecues were 'not her style,' and she was adamant that one of Dante's lawyer friends or a business associate would be much more appropriate as best man.

Finally she had agreed to attend—but only if they went immediately, so that they would still have time to have dinner at their favourite restaurant. This was news to Dante, who hadn't even known they *had* a favourite restaurant!

Ellen had carried on in the same vein for the hour it had taken to get here, and Dante had switched off and let her chatter. But when he had glanced across to where Mike had indicated his brother and seen the woman with him he'd immediately switched on again.

Now Dante studied the tall, striking redhead at Tony's side. There was something about her that niggled at him. He had caught the name Beth, but he could not remember having met anyone called Beth before. Yet there was definitely something familiar about her. Then, as the sun's rays caught her hair, turning it to flame, it came to him—she was the stunning woman he had noticed in the street a few days ago.

Dante barely heard the conversation that continued. His dark gaze roamed over her instead. He noticed the swell of her breasts beneath the lemon silk shirt she wore tucked into white jeans that moulded her slim hips and long legs, before his gaze slid back to trace the creamy skin over the high cheekbones of her face, framed by the red hair that was styled to fall sleekly to her shoulders. Finally his look rested on her big green eyes. He was intrigued as to who she was, and what she was to Tony.

'Beth—my brother Dante.'

Tony made the introduction and Beth had no excuse but to finally look at Cannavaro.

Dante offered his hand. 'It is a pleasure to meet you, Beth.' Her eyes were cold, he noted, and the fingers that briefly touched his and swiftly withdrew were smooth and cool. But the heated sensation he felt at her merest touch surprised him—and her, it would seem. He recognised the flash of awareness in her green eyes though she fought to disguise it. Her lashes flickered down and her full lips tightened. He sensed her antagonism. She had not wanted to shake his hand. Only social niceties had demanded the slight contact.

Dante wasn't a conceited man, but her reaction wasn't the one he usually got from females. This woman had never met him but she was determined not to like him, and he had to wonder why.

'Nice to meet you,' Beth said, but she refused to use

his name. Her fingers stung from the brief contact with his and she took a step back, shocked that he could affect her so intensely. His powerful physical presence provoked an instant reaction—a stomach-churning anger that she was barely able to control.

'I'm considering following you, Dante.' Tony reached his arm around Beth again, holding her close. 'And talking Beth into marrying me. What do you think?' he asked outrageously.

Beth's startled gaze flew to Tony. What on earth was he playing at?

'Beth is a lovely girl, I'm sure,' Dante offered with a cynical smile.

He had met a lot of women in his time, and could see the beautiful Beth was probably older than Tony— maybe not so much in years, but, by the guarded look about her, certainly in experience. She could be more interested in Tony's money than she was in the man. His brother worked in the merchant bank his father, Harry, owned and stood to inherit a fortune. The fact that he chose to share an apartment with Mike in suburbia, rather than a luxury apartment he could easily afford in the city centre, didn't mean Beth did not know exactly who Tony was—an extremely good catch for any woman.

Beth's blood ran cold as Dante's hard dark eyes met hers. Now she recognised the cynicism in his smile immediately—but years ago she had not, and it had been her downfall. Her anger and resentment grew at the memory as he continued speaking.

'But you have only just turned twenty-three, Tony. Isn't that a bit young to be contemplating matrimony?' Dante queried. He had seen the anger in Beth's eyes and his conviction that she was only after Tony's money deepened. This woman was smart enough to know that as the older brother he was a possible threat to her plan. 'Marriage is an expensive business—especially for a young man just starting his career. I'm sure Beth would agree.'

His mocking tone did nothing to quell the bitterness bubbling inside Beth. No wonder Tony wanted to get one over on the arrogant swine. Rashly, she decided to help him. 'Oh, I don't know. Money isn't everything.' She shot Cannavaro a defiant glance before looking adoringly up at Tony. 'Is it, darling?'

'You've got that spot-on,' Tony offered, his eyes dancing with amusement as he planted a brief kiss on her lips. 'Isn't she incredible, bro?' he prompted.

'Yes,' Dante agreed curtly, surprised by the swift flare of irritation he felt at seeing them kiss. His dark gaze flicked to Beth and he caught the gleam in her green eyes. It wasn't passion for Tony, he recognised, but a direct challenge aimed at *him*.

There was nothing Dante liked better than a challenge, and there was something about the striking redhead that had aroused his suspicions the minute he had met her. Now he was in danger of arousing another part of him, and worryingly it had nothing to do with his fiancée. He hadn't reacted to a woman so swiftly in a long time. He enjoyed sex, but was never blinded by it, and he chose his partners carefully—as he had Ellen. He was always in total control, as he was in all aspects of his life. Yet every instinct he possessed was telling him his surprising reaction to Beth was not just sexual attraction. It was as though he knew her—but how?

He needed time to think, and changed the subject.

'What about a drink, Tony? This is supposed to be a party. I'll have a soft drink as I'm driving.' And, concentrating on his fiancée, he added, 'A vodka and tonic all right for you, Ellen?'

'I'll get them, Tony,' Beth offered, her heart pounding in panic as she realised that playing along with Tony's game to irritate his brother had been the height of stupidity. She had let her anger overcome her caution and drawn attention to herself—a big mistake. 'You stay with your guests. You must have a lot to talk about with a family wedding coming up.'

Tony kissed her cheek and let her go. 'Thanks, you're a gem. And bring me a beer as well, hmm?'

Beth agreed, and with a huge sense of relief walked across to get a can of beer, then sprinted up the stairs of the boys' apartment and into the kitchen.

She recognised a couple of their friends from the bank, and responding to their chatter helped her to regain her shattered nerves as she mixed the drinks and placed them on a tray. Caution and confidence, she reminded herself. But even so she was in no hurry to go back down to the party.

Just then Mike appeared. 'I need more food! These people eat like horses,' he declared, and she saw a lifeline.

'You're looking stressed, Mike.' And, handing him the tray, she suggested, 'Why don't you add a drink for yourself and take these down to Tony, relax and enjoy the party? I'll take care of the barbecue—no problem.'

'You are an angel.' He grinned and agreed.

Beth doubted Cannavaro and Ellen would deign to eat from the barbecue. Fine dining was more their thing, and she could hopefully avoid them for the rest of the evening.

* * *

Tony had watched Beth depart with an appreciative eye, then turned to catch Dante doing the same. 'So, when are you getting married, bro?' he asked mischievously. 'At your age you don't want to hang around.'

Before Dante could reply Ellen laughed and launched into a long explanation as to how difficult it was to get the right church at the right time and find the right venue for the reception. He saw Tony's eyes glaze over with drink or boredom—more likely the latter—and he knew the feeling.

Dante had presumed that once they were engaged all he'd have to do was pay up and turn up on the wedding day. The endless lists and arrangements Ellen expected him to be interested in and discuss had come as an unpleasant shock to him.

Eventually Ellen ended with a date in September.

'That's fine,' Tony said. 'Don't forget to send me an invite. I'll bring Beth. Hopefully it will encourage her down the same path.'

'Is that wise? The guests will be family and close friends, and though Beth seems nice how long have you known her?' Dante demanded. Somehow the thought of the emerald-eyed beauty as a guest at his wedding was not one he wanted to contemplate.

'Ever since we moved in, eighteen months ago. She's a great girl and a fabulous cook. Her cakes are to die for. I don't know what we'd do without her. Isn't that right?' Tony asked as Mike appeared with the drinks.

'Yes, she is a diamond—especially to you, mate. And as we're standing in *her* garden, and *she* prepared most of the food and has offered to take over the barbecue so I can enjoy myself, I'd say she is indispensable. And she certainly improves the view....'

Dante had wondered why Tony insisted on living out here, and now he knew. Tony was infatuated by the woman. With a few judicious questions Dante soon found out a lot more about Beth Lazenby. She was twenty-seven, and an accountant for a prestigious firm in the centre of London. She owned a cottage by the sea, and lived in the ground-floor apartment—too close to Tony for Dante's comfort. He wasn't sure why, but his gut feeling was telling him there was a lot more to Beth than met the eye.

He glanced across to the barbecue and saw her standing there, handing out plates of food to a group of men gathered around her, none of whom could take their eyes off her. Maybe that was the problem. She was tall, and so stunningly attractive few men would think to look past her surface beauty. She was an unlikely accountant. With her height and looks she could have been a model—she was slender enough. But maybe her high, firm breasts were a little too much for a fashion model, he mused.

'Dante, darling.'

Ellen's voice stopped his musing.

'I feel like dancing.' Grasping his arm, she smiled up at him.

'Not my kind of dancing, but I'll give it a go.'

Ellen was the lovely, intelligent woman whom he had chosen to be his wife, Dante reminded himself, and it was time he stopped worrying about the redhead and concentrated on his fiancée. Ellen had not wanted to attend this barbecue, but she was making an effort for his sake. Dancing with her was the least he could do....

* * *

Julian, the last man standing by the barbecue, was talking about stockbroking, laughing as he described his latest gamble on the markets. Beth listened politely, her mind only partially on what he said. She seemed unable to stop her eyes from straying towards the people dancing on the patio, and the tallest man in particular. For a big man he was a smooth mover—though he wasn't so much dancing as allowing his fiancée to flit adoringly around him. More fool her, Beth thought. In her experience most men were a waste of time. All she wanted to do was call it a night, get into her apartment and check on Binkie. But there was no way she was going to walk through the crowd of gyrating bodies.

Luckily the music stopped and Mike came strolling over, his face flushed and smiling, obviously having enjoyed himself. 'Sorry, Beth. I didn't mean to leave you so long, but with it still being so light I didn't realise the time. Tony has just gone to change the music. You go and enjoy yourself, and I'll pack up here.'

For Beth it already felt like the longest night of her life, and she leapt at the chance to escape. People were moving to replenish their drinks, and her route was almost clear to her back door.

She was nearly there when the music started again— this time slow and moody—and suddenly her way was blocked as Cannavaro stepped in front of her, crowding her. She wanted to step back, but her pride would not let her.

'May I have this dance? Tony is partnering Ellen, and it will give us a chance to get to know each other. We might all be family one day.'

Beth tensed and looked up at him—which was an

unusual event in itself for her. She noticed that his eyes
were not black. They were the colour of molasses—dark
and golden. She found herself thinking that once she
fell into them she would be stuck for ever. Disturbed
by the fanciful thought, she caught the gleam of mockery in those same eyes and wanted to refuse his request
outright. But she did not dare. He had not recognised
her, she was sure, but she had aroused his suspicion by
being less than courteous when they had been introduced. She did not want to compound her mistake by
showing her dislike again.

She took a deep breath. 'That's not likely to happen.
Tony was just teasing,' she managed to say evenly. 'But,
yes, if you insist, I will dance with you.'

'Oh, I insist, Beth.' He drawled her name softly and
his arm slid around her waist.

He looked at her, his other hand taking hers, and she
was not prepared for the tingling sensation that crept
over her skin and made her shiver as he held her close
to his long body.

A reaction to the cooling night air, she told herself,
but somehow her body, with a will of its own, was moving with him, automatically following his movements.

'You are a very lovely lady, Beth. What man wouldn't
insist?' he added in that deep, barely accented silken
voice she remembered so well and so bitterly.

She forgot her good intentions. 'Are you trying to
flirt with me, Mr Cannavaro?' she demanded. 'And
you an engaged man,' she prompted, giving him a de-
risory smile while trying to control her inexplicably
racing pulse.

A quizzical expression flickered across his face for
a moment, and his incredible eyes seemed to bore into

hers as his hand stroked up her spine to hold her closer still. To her shame she felt a fullness in her breasts when they came in contact with his broad chest.

'No, Beth. I was stating the truth. But if I *was* flirting with you I would not have to try very hard,' Dante opined, fully appreciating the feminine sway of her shapely body against his own, testing his control to the limit. 'I felt you tremble when I took you in my arms, and sensed it in the softening of your body against mine. There is an instant sexual attraction between us—unfortunate, but true. Under the circumstances it is obviously not to be acted upon. But I also sense something more. You seem afraid of me—even actively to dislike me—and I have to wonder why. Are you sure we have not met before?'

God, he analysed everything, and talked like a lawyer even as they moved to the music. His muscular thighs brushed against hers, raising her temperature, and it took all her nerve to hold his dark gaze.

'I shivered because it is getting cooler now,' she lied. 'And, no, we have never met before. I didn't even know Tony had a brother. He never mentioned you until you turned up here in the garden.'

Dante stilled and let Beth take a step back, putting space between them. His heavy-lidded eyes were shrewd and penetrating, and swept over her flushed defiant face before moving lower.

'Interesting if true!' He raised a sardonic eyebrow, noting the thrust of her nipples against her shirt.

The lovely Beth was definitely lying about one part of that statement. He had met enough females in his time, and was experienced enough to recognise when a lustful attraction was mutual. But was she lying about not knowing Tony had a brother until tonight? She had not said *half-brother,* and if she was telling the truth surely she would naturally assume his name was Hetherington, the same as Tony's? And yet she had called him Mr Cannavaro—even though his name had not been mentioned when the introductions had been made. He doubted Tony, who was not into formality of any kind, would have called him anything but Dante or bro in the couple of minutes before they had been introduced. So how could she know his surname unless she *had* met him before, or at least heard of him?

The mystery of Beth Lazenby deepened. His legal instincts told him she was hiding something—but what? And in that moment Dante decided to make it his business to discover everything about her. Not for himself, but to protect his brother, of course.

A wave of heat swept through Beth at his intense scrutiny and it took every scrap of willpower she possessed to control her traitorous body. But at least she was saved from having to respond as Tony and Ellen appeared.

'One fiancée returned to you, bro, worn out from dancing with me—or it could be the vodka I gave her. She wants to go home.' Tony grinned, swaying on his feet, and Beth grabbed his arm to steady him. He had definitely had too much to drink.

'Thanks a bunch, Tony,' Dante said dryly, his expression grim as he wrapped his arm around a slightly glassy-eyed Ellen. And with a goodnight and a curt nod to Beth, much to her relief he left.

Beth took the key from her back pocket and, ignoring Tony's drunken request to dance, slipped into her apartment and locked the door behind her. She fell back against it, breathing deeply, fighting to regain her composure.

Binkie appeared and she picked him up in her arms and carried him through into the living room. Her knees weak, with a sigh she sank down onto the sofa, cuddling the cat on her lap, her mind in turmoil as the significance of Cannavaro being Tony's brother sank in.

Everyone had bad days, she reminded herself, but today hers had gone from good straight to diabolical. She glanced around the cosy room that was her sanctuary, her gaze resting on the two photographs in identical silver frames on the mantelpiece. One was of the parents she had adored, and the other of Helen, her dearest friend. All three were dead now, and moisture glazed her eyes.

Clive Hampton, Helen's lawyer, whom Beth now considered a friend and mentor, was the closest thing she had to family. He had been instrumental in getting her a job in the offices of a local accountancy firm, where she had got the opportunity to train in-house as an accountant. After taking the requisite exams over two years she had eventually become qualified.

She spoke to Clive frequently on the telephone, and often visited him at his home in Richmond. She was meeting him tomorrow for Sunday lunch, and had almost forgotten in the trauma of the evening. He was over sixty now, and thinking of retiring soon, and though she talked to him about most things, telling him how she felt about Cannavaro was not one of them. It was much too personal. She had never even told Helen how badly the man had affected her in court, only that he was clever and that her lawyer, Miss Sims, had been useless against him. No, this latest development she had to take care of herself.

Her time in prison had taught her how to build a protective shell around her emotions and present a blank face in front of warders and prisoners alike. Living in a confined environment and sharing communal showers had come as a shock, but she had quickly realised that women came in all shapes and sizes and soon thought nothing of stripping off in front of anyone. She told herself she was no better or worse than anyone else, but all her life she had always felt the odd one out and that hadn't changed. And with her new identity she was even more wary of making friends.

Tony and Mike were the only friends she had in London, though she had quite a few in Faith Cove.

Wearily she let her head fall back on the sofa and closed her eyes. She had never felt as alone as she did now. Not since that fatal day eight years ago when she had stood in the dock, trembling with fear. And the same hateful arrogant man was responsible.... In her head she wished she had the nerve to tell Dante Cannavaro exactly what she thought of him, but in reality she knew she could not.

He was a dangerously clever man: she trembled if he so much as touched her and he already thought they had met before. She was not going to take the chance of him remembering where... Not that it would matter if he did, but she did not need the aggravation in her life. What she needed to do was make sure she never met him again, and if that meant moving she would. Tony had said he hadn't seen his brother since last year, so with luck she'd have some time to decide.

Binkie stirred and stretched on her lap. Sighing, Beth

got to her feet. 'Come on, Binkie. I can see you want feeding, and then I am going to bed.'

But once she was in bed disturbing thoughts of Dante Cannavaro filled her mind. The first time she had seen him across the courtroom she had felt an instant connection with him. Her stomach had churned and her heart had leapt and naively she had thought he was her savior. But he had betrayed her. Again tonight he'd ignited those same sensations in her, but she told herself that this time it was anger and hatred for the man.

Yet, as she tossed and turned, hot and restless beneath the coverlet, remembering the strength of his arms holding her as they danced, the heat of his long body moving her to the music, she had the growing suspicion that he could be right. Never in her life had she responded to any man the way she did to Cannavaro. She had met plenty of men in the last few years, and quite a lot had asked her for a date, but she could count on one hand the rare occasions she had accepted.

For all the harm Cannavaro had done to her, could her intense awareness of him, the rush of sensations he aroused in her, be purely sexual, as he said, and not just hatred as she believed? She saw in her mind's eye his broodingly handsome face, the compelling dark eyes, and a shiver quivered through her body. How could she know for sure?

The first boy she had kissed had been the slimy liar Timothy Bewick, and when Cannavaro had questioned her at the trial he had implied their kiss had been a lot more. She hadn't recognised the *femme fatale* he had made her out to be, but the jury had believed him.

By the time Beth had got out of prison she'd been determined to allow no man to get close to her. Her friend

Helen had still been in prison, serving a twenty-year sentence for killing her bully of an ex-husband. Helen had spent years living with his violent rages, and it had only been when she had seen his anger directed at their daughter, Vicky, that Helen had found the courage to divorce him. Five years later Vicky had died while staying at her father's holiday villa in Spain. According to her father, Vicky had slipped and cracked her head open. The Spanish authorities had believed him. But Helen had known he'd finally gone too far and she'd snapped, deliberately running him down with her Land Rover outside his London home.

Helen had told Beth her story, and told her to look around at the rest of the women they'd shared the prison with. Most of the women had been there because of a man. A man who'd told them what to do, whether they were thieves, prostitutes, drug mules or anything else. And they'd done it because they'd been deluded enough to believe the man loved them. In Helen's case she had let grief and hatred of her ex take over, and in destroying his life had destroyed her own too. Helen had warned her never to let any man take over *her* life.

Helen's words of wisdom still held true, and they strengthened Beth's resolve to put as much distance between herself and Dante Cannavaro as she possibly could.

In a moment of insight Beth realised that her cottage in the village of Faith Cove was the only place she felt truly herself.

When Beth finally fell into a restless sleep the nightmare she had not suffered from for a long time returned with a vengeance—only the ending wasn't the same. She was in the dock, with a big handsome man in black tormenting her, twisting every word she said. Then he was smiling, his deep voice and dark eyes drawing her in. And then the nightmare turned into an erotic dream of strong arms holding her, firm, sensuous lips kissing her, hands caressing her, thrilling her.

She cried out and woke up, hot and moist between her thighs and with her heart pounding like a drum.

The next day Beth drove to Richmond for Sunday lunch with Clive, and discussed with him what she had been thinking of doing since the last time she had stayed at the cottage. With Clive's full approval Beth made the decision to leave London.

She was going to move to Faith Cove and refurbish the cottage Helen had gifted to her in her will. Ironically, Helen's brute of a husband, never thinking his wife would have the nerve to divorce him, had put the cottage in Helen's name to avoid tax when he had bought the house fifteen years earlier. When she *had* divorced him there had been nothing he could do about her keeping it.

Now Beth had plans for the cottage. Although 'cottage' was actually a misnomer, as the place was really a large house with six bedrooms, often rented out to families. First she would convert the roof space of the multi-car garage at the rear of the property into a three-roomed apartment. That way she could carry on renting out the house as a holiday let while living permanently either in the apartment or the house when it was vacant. Beth was sure she could make a comfortable living out of it, and she could continue as an accountant for private clients. Maybe she could even convert part of the garage into a surfers' shop later, which would give her even more independence and ensure she could stay away from the man who haunted her dreams.

Dante Cannavaro, with a face like thunder, walked into his office on Monday morning, sat down at his desk and contacted the security firm he used when a delicate investigation was needed for a client.

Minutes later he lounged back in his black leather chair, his mind not on work but fixated on a tall redhead. He had put the wheels in motion to find out exactly who Beth Lazenby was, and if there was anything suspicious about her he would deal with her appropriately.

Miss Lazenby had already messed up his weekend and a hell of a lot more—including his plans for the future. He had taken Ellen back to her apartment on Saturday night, but had not joined her in bed because she had obviously drunk too much. Ellen had taken offence, blaming Dante for taking her to Tony's party in the first place, and not taking her out to dinner. She had accused Dante of being arrogant and uncaring and of eyeing up another woman in her presence—namely Beth. She had claimed that he did not love her and had used a lot of words he had never thought she knew. The argument had culminated in Ellen calling the wedding off and throwing her ring at him as he had exited her apartment.

Dante had returned home in a foul mood, and had then spent a restless night with the image of a flame-haired woman plaguing his mind and his body. He'd had to remind himself that he had gotten over the urge to bed every desirable woman he met years ago. Yet he was still convinced that he knew Beth…. But how and from where he had no idea—and that was his problem.

Dante was as frustrated as hell, thanks to the red-headed witch, and he was damn sure he was not going to let her mess up Tony's life. He glanced at his watch. He had a flight booked to New York at noon, and he expected to be there for a few weeks at least. He called his driver to pick him up and got to his feet, a ruthless gleam in his dark eyes.

When he returned to England, whatever the outcome of his enquiries, he would take great pleasure in dealing with Beth Lazenby personally. There was no way she was marrying Tony! Just the thought of being faced with Beth as his brother's wife at every family gathering for the rest of his life was enough to make him shudder.

About to get in the car, he stopped and took his cell phone from his pocket and called Tony, realising his younger brother was impulsive enough to marry the woman without a second thought. Proof or not, it was his brotherly duty to warn Tony of his suspicions for his own good

'Dante—to what do I owe this honor?' Tony answered. 'You rarely call me—and never during working hours.'

'I want to let you know Ellen and I have split up. The wedding is cancelled and I am going to America for a while.'

'Sorry, but I can't say I'm surprised. In fact I told Beth I was amazed you'd got engaged in the first place. Why settle for one when you can take your pick, bro?'

Dante heard his chuckle and grimaced. 'Yes, well, I've learned my lesson. But knowing how impulsive you can be, I thought I should warn you in case you make the same mistake.'

'Warn me? That sounds ominous.'

'Not ominous, just cautious… I've met Beth's type before—a beautiful woman who probably knows your father owns a bank and is as interested in money as she is in you.' Dante heard Tony laugh out loud and gritted his teeth. His brother never took anything seriously.

'Ah, Dante, you really are too serious to be believed. As for Beth—I really couldn't care less if she knows Dad owns a bank or not. You've met her. She is absolutely gorgeous! Do you honestly think I, or any other red-blooded male who was lucky enough to have Beth in his bed, would give a damn about the money? You must really be getting old, Dante, but don't worry—I won't do anything you wouldn't do…. *Ciao.*' And, still laughing, he clicked off.

Dante slipped his phone back into his pocket, feeling a complete idiot. Tony's parting shot *did* worry him, and as he got into the car, his lips twisting wryly, he acknowledged that his brother's assessment of the male of the species where Beth Lazenby was concerned was probably correct.

CHAPTER THREE

IT WAS A blazing-hot day, and Beth's carefully straightened hair was already beginning to wave in the heat as she searched the kitchen one more time.

'Got you!' she cried triumphantly and, cradling Binkie in her arms, she carried him into the hall and closed the kitchen door with her hip. Finally she was ready to go. Her luggage was loaded into the boot of her car, and had been for hours, but Binkie was not. It was a five-hour drive to Devon, and she had planned on leaving at one. It was now three, but with luck she would easily make it before dark.

She eyed the cat carrier standing open in the hall. Binkie hated travelling, which was why she had spent ages trying to coax him out from under the kitchen units, after having chased him around the garden and the apartment. Now all she had to do was put him in the carrier and they could go.

Beth had given in her notice at work on Monday and, with the three weeks' holiday she had yet to take, did not need to return to the office. She had spoken to Tony last night, but had not mentioned she was leaving permanently. She intended to do that when she came back to clear her apartment. Tony had promised to keep an eye on the place, and had also told her his brother's engagement was off. Dante had gone to work in America for a while, conveniently escaping the flak from their mother over the cancelled wedding. She had already bought a hat!

Tony's news had been music to Beth's ears, and she'd realised she had probably worried unnecessarily. But she was pleased that Dante's appearance in her life again had focused her mind and forced her to make a decision. Now, sun, sea and a new chapter in her life beckoned, Beth thought happily, bending down to lower Binkie into the carrier—which was easier said than done. He had leapt out of it twice already.

'Stop wriggling, you useless ball of fur,' she told him, and was just about to draw one hand free to shut the carrier when there was a ring at the front door— peremptory and sharp.

Ignoring it, Beth leant over, using her body to block Binkie's escape, and swiftly closed the lid.

'All right, all right—I'm coming!' she yelled as the bell rang again and kept on ringing.

She got to her feet and, leaving the carrier on the floor, walked to the door. Probably some salesman, she thought. But whoever it was she would get rid of them quickly. She opened the door.

The social smile froze on her lips and she simply stared at the man standing before her. A dark, unsmiling figure in a charcoal pinstriped suit, jacket unfastened, the white shirt beneath open at the neck and startlingly brilliant against his tanned throat. Her stomach clenched and she stiffened, straightening her shoulders. It was the man she hated with a passion but had dreamed of far too often in the past two weeks for her peace of mind. Cannavaro...

Dante had received the report on Beth Lazenby a week ago in New York, and what he had read had confirmed his suspicions about her. He had arrived back in London this morning, and after a shower and a change had leapt in his car and driven here. Now he was on her doorstep. His features hardened as slowly he took in every detail of the way she looked: her hair was dishevelled, her face clear of make-up—and as for what she was wearing...

If he'd had the slightest doubt of the investigator's findings that Jane Mason and Beth Lazenby were one and the same, it vanished as he noted the snug fit of denim shorts that showed off her long legs and the skimpy white top that revealed a tantalising cleavage and stopped six inches short of the toned flesh of a slender waist and abdomen. She was slimmer than before, but still had curves in all the right places, and she was more striking than ever.

He felt a surge of lust and saw again in his mind's eye the image of that girl in the picture, wearing almost the same outfit as this woman wore now, but with one dramatic difference. The girl in the picture had had long black hair—as had the girl who'd stood in the dock and been found guilty of being a drug dealer.

He had been right to be suspicious of the redheaded beauty who had captivated his brother. She had latched on to a younger boy when she was a teenager, and been prepared to use his infatuation for her to ruin him and save her own neck when she had been caught in her reckless drug dealing. It would seem that she had ensnared his younger brother in much the same way. She obviously had not changed—only in the colour of her hair, which couldn't be real. The thing that surprised him was that he had not recognised who she was sooner.

'Hello, Beth. Or should I say Jane?' he queried sardonically.

'My legal name is Beth Lazenby,' Beth stated bluntly.

The air between them was crackling with tension.

'Maybe now. But it wasn't when you were in the dock at nineteen.'

'You've finally recognised me. Bully for you,' she snapped sarcastically, seeing no point in denying it. So he had remembered where he had seen her before? Her temper rose at the audacity of the man, confronting her on her own doorstep.

'Not exactly. But the investigator I hired to check on you refreshed my memory.'

Beth's temper very nearly exploded at that revelation, and only by a terrific effort of will did she control the anger simmering inside her—along with other emotions she refused to recognise. She reminded herself she was no longer a gullible teenager but a confident woman, and she flatly refused to let Cannavaro intimidate her again.

'Shame you wasted your money. I'm going on holiday now, and have already spent ages chasing the cat—which has made me late. You need to leave.' And she caught the door handle with the intention of slamming the door in his face.

'Not so fast.' He put his foot in the door. 'I want to talk to you.'

'Well, tough. Because I have absolutely nothing to say to you.' She turned, hanging on to her temper by a thread, and went to retrieve the cat in order to go.

But, remembering the time and pain Cannavaro had already cost her, she decided she had nothing left to lose, and spun back to find him towering over her.

She looked up at him, her green eyes spitting fury. 'Except to say you have some nerve investigating me. Call yourself a lawyer? You are without doubt the most arrogant, devious, manipulative, lying bastard it has ever been my misfortune to meet. Got it? Now, go.'

His face was like carved granite and his eyes hard as he watched her mouth spew out the angry words. Suddenly he moved and a long arm shot around her. His large hand splayed across her back whilst the other grasped the back of her head and jerked her body towards him. He dipped his head, his mouth crashing down on hers, relentlessly prising her lips apart with the powerful thrust of his tongue. Shocked and furious, she tried to pull away, but his hands clamped her in position. Her head was so close to his she could not drag it from beneath his all-consuming mouth. The steel band of his arm was holding her pressed hard against his long body. She tried to struggle, but he was too strong—and shamefully, instead of feeling revulsion, she was floundering in the wave of heady sensation flowing through her body.

Frantically she tried to lift her hands and shove him away, but she was held so tightly against the hard wall of his chest that all she could do was claw at his broad shoulders as he wreaked sensual havoc with his penetrating kiss. Still she tried to resist, but he explored her mouth, hotly igniting a flame of arousal deep inside that scorched through her defences—and suddenly she wasn't clawing, but clinging to him.

His fingers wound into her hair, pulling it back to

tilt her head to one side, his mouth trailing the line of her neck to suck on the frantically leaping pulse there.

This could not be! She hated the man. She began to struggle so wildly that their bodies swayed and crashed against the wall, his long, hard length pinning her there. She was aware of his hot, male scent and the strength of his muscular and highly aroused body against her own in a shockingly intimate way she had never experienced before.

He lifted his head, her breath catching as she saw his face. He was staring at her with dark, mesmerising eyes as his hand moved from her head to the neckline of her top, his long fingers slipping beneath the fabric to graze a swelling nipple. Involuntarily her body arched, and she bit back the moan that rose in her throat.

Her voice seemed to have deserted her, and her heart was thudding so hard she thought it might burst. Her passionate hatred of him had been overtaken by passionate desire.

'You can't help yourself. You want me,' he said in a deep, thickened voice.

'No, I hate you,' she said hoarsely.

He gave her one long look, his face suddenly wearing a cold remoteness that was frightening in itself. He straightened up and pulled her closer against him, his hand circling her throat to tip her head back. 'Hate away. But think yourself lucky I only kissed you. If any man had said what you did to me he would be on the floor now. I will not tolerate anyone defaming my character—and certainly not a conniving ex-con like you. Understand?'

Shaken, and battling to control her overloaded senses, she heard his words and they were better than

a cold shower. How typical of the arrogant devil. Beth
shook her head in disgust.

'Now we will have that talk.' His hands dropped
from her and he took a step back—and stumbled over
the cat carrier. He swore, and Binkie shot out beneath
his feet. Dante struggled to avoid the cat, lost the battle,
and fell to the floor.

Beth laughed—if a bit hysterically. Perfect karma,
she thought. The stunned look on his handsome face
was priceless.

'How the mighty are fallen,' she quipped, and bent
down to grab Binkie, ignoring the furious mountain of
a man leaping to his feet. 'There, there, Binkie,' Beth
said as she walked into the living room, cuddling the
cat over her chest and shoulder to comfort him—and to
disguise her tight nipples. 'I know the nasty man kicked
you, but he's going now.'

Dante straightened up, not quite sure what had just
happened. He'd been kissing her like a savage beast
gone wild one minute, the next on the floor in a heap!
He could still taste her on his tongue, and Beth—Jane—
whoever she was—had for the first time in his life left
him knocked out sensually and physically.

'I did not kick the cat,' Dante declared, following
her into the room. His pride was seriously dented and
he raked a distracted hand though his hair. What *was*
it about this witch of a woman that turned him into a
primitive, clumsy oaf? He had never tripped over his
feet since he was a child. He looked at her, with a great
lump of red fur the same colour as her hair clamped to
her chest, her slender fingers stroking the cat's head,
then moving to scratch the animal under the chin.

She raised her eyes and looked at him. 'You kicked

over his carrier with him inside, which is the same thing—isn't it, Binkie?'

Dante could not believe she had actually asked the damned cat. Maybe he had fallen into a different dimension. Maybe she really was a witch and the cat was her familiar, he thought, as two identical pairs of green eyes stared accusingly at him. The cat bared its teeth and he was sure he heard it hiss in agreement with his mistress.

He shook his head to clear his brain. The woman was driving him crazy. What hope would his impressionable young brother have with her? None—and his express purpose for being here was to get her out of Tony's life.

'I am not going anywhere—and neither are you until we talk,' he commanded between clenched teeth. To emphasise the fact he shrugged off his jacket, crossed to one of the sofas flanking the fireplace and dropped it on the arm before he sat down.

Beth was a realist. She had to be. She saw the cold determination in his hard face. The wild, passionate interlude in the hall had been exactly what he had said—a punishment for daring to impugn his good character. Which was a joke, because as far as *she* was concerned he didn't have one.

'I'll give you five minutes,' she stated, her lips twitching as she sat down on the opposite sofa. She kissed the cat and put him down beside her. 'Go on, Binkie. You can have another roam around the kitchen before we leave.' She watched him jump off the sofa.

'Do you always talk to your cat?'

She turned her cool gaze on Dante, trying to ignore the lingering warmth in the rest of her body that wasn't being helped by the sight of him in a tailored white shirt and pleated trousers that fitted snugly over his muscular thighs. 'Not always, but he is one of the few honest males I have met, and he is a great judge of character.' She glanced down at Binkie, who had walked straight across to Cannavaro with his back arched, fur bristling as though he was about to attack. 'He certainly recognises *your* type,' she said dryly.

'That cat does not like me.' Dante stated the obvious, eyeing the hunchbacked animal with equal dislike. He was amazed to see that at the sound of his mistress's voice the cat turned and looked at Beth, then crossed to rub slowly up against her bare legs before walking out of the door.

She shrugged her shoulders 'Binkie is a tomcat and you are a strange male invading his territory. His natural instinct is to protect it.'

'Not that strange. I have known you a long time, Jane.' He deliberately used her old name, determined to get down to business.

Beth let her eyes rest on him for a moment. He was sitting on her sofa, making himself at home, with his long legs stretched out in casual ease, his black hair falling over his brow. He seemed so supremely sure of himself. To her shame, Beth felt her body responding to his potent masculine appeal and anger resurfaced— almost as much with herself as him.

'If you think by calling me Jane you can intimidate me, forget it,' she said bluntly. 'I am no longer an innocent teenager you can browbeat in the dock.'

A black brow arched sardonically. 'Innocent! I seem to recall it was the jury's unanimous opinion that you were one hundred percent guilty.'

'You mean the opinion *you* talked them into believing?'

'What's that supposed to mean?' His brow lifted again. There was no sign of conscience on his face.

Beth shook her head dismissively. What was the point in arguing with him? She had lost eighteen months of her life because of Cannavaro and she wasn't wasting any more. Rising to her feet, she deliberately let her gaze roam over his darkly attractive face, broad shoulders and the glimpse of black body hair revealed by the open-necked shirt before moving it lower over his long body....

He was a supreme physical specimen of masculinity, with the ability to arouse any woman, and her own innate honesty forced her to admit she was no exception. He had been right about the attraction between them. Even now, angry as she was, she could feel the sexual tension shimmering. But it didn't make him any less of a lying toad in her eyes.

'My name is Beth. You are in my home uninvited, supposedly because you want to talk, but so far I have heard nothing that I have not heard before. So get on with it. No thanks to you, I *do* have a life to get on with.' She deliberately glanced down at her wristwatch and back up to him, her green eyes clashing with his. 'You have two minutes, then I am leaving.'

'You are very confident for an ex-con. But will you be so confident when I tell Tony of your past, I wonder?' he drawled, lounging back against the soft cushions, obviously not about to move. 'I recognised the type of woman you are the first time I saw you in the dock. You would do anything—even try to destroy a young boy who's infatuated by you—to save your own skin. Now you have Tony equally infatuated with you and wanting to marry you, for no other reason than just because you can or—more likely—you want him for his wealth.'

That made Beth smile. 'Not very flattering to your brother, are you? But feel free to tell him. I don't mind, I don't think Tony would either. A lot of young men his age consider it really cool to have a girlfriend who has done time in jail.'

His dark eyes watched her penetratingly and she knew she had got to him.

'You could be right. But, believe me, I do not make idle threats. You will move out of this apartment and leave Tony alone—no contact of any kind—or I will tell your employer exactly who you are: a convicted drug dealer who has spent eighteen months in prison. I'm sure that's something you probably missed off your CV. Steel and White is a highly respectable firm and will take a dim view of the omission. You will be out of a job—your carefully crafted reputation ruined.'

Beth listened to him with rising anger, realising he must have had her investigated immediately after the barbecue—otherwise he would know she had given in her notice to Steel and White on Monday. She did not know much about men, but she wasn't a fool. The way Cannavaro had treated her earlier in the hall had surprised and aroused her, but there was no disguising the fact that he had been equally aroused—and she seriously doubted he was doing this just for his brother!

This man had destroyed her once and he was trying to do so again. But he wasn't quite as clever as he thought. Prison life had taught her to control her body and her temper rigorously, but she could not resist goading the sanctimonious jerk.

'That could happen, I suppose,' she agreed, without

batting an eyelash. 'But I am a good accountant, and there are plenty of other jobs. Or I could set up my own business. You obviously haven't thought this through, because short of following me around for the rest of my life there is nothing much you can do to me. According to you, I committed a crime—but I have served my time and am now a reformed character. So I changed my name by deed poll? That is perfectly legal. And for over six years now I have led a perfectly honest life. Can you say the same? I doubt it,' she said derisively. 'As for your threats—they don't bother me. Thanks to you I grew a thick skin in prison, and I don't have to do a damn thing you say. But, if it helps, I have no intention of marrying your brother—or any other man for that matter. Now, your two minutes are up. Time to go.'

He rose to his feet. She thought for a moment she had won, and turned towards the door, but a large hand clamped around her upper arm and spun her back to face him.

'Not so fast,' Dante declared, uncomfortably aware that the words of her spirited response was true. His investigator's report had confirmed she had led a blameless life since her release from prison, but it did not make her any less guilty of the crime in his eyes. However, it did make him think again about what he was about to say. He studied her from beneath narrowed lids, noting the slight flush that stained her cheeks and the glitter of anger in her huge green eyes as she glared up at him. He was struck by her bravery in trying to defy him—but not enough to change his mind and let her go. And it had absolutely nothing to do with the growing ache in his groin!

'This conversation is not over yet, Beth. I didn't get

around to mentioning your good friend Clive Hampton—the lawyer of your old cell mate, I believe.'

Beth stilled. 'Clive?' she murmured, and despite her brave words she suddenly felt wary.

'He is a fine lawyer, known for his charity work and nearing retirement. There are rumours he will receive a decoration in the New Year's Honours list.' His eyes watched her. 'Such a shame if his reputation is destroyed by his friendship with you. Maybe he could even be disbarred by the Law Lords.'

'No...' she breathed. 'You can't do that. Clive is the most caring, honest man I know. He has never broken a law in his life, I'm sure.'

'He doesn't have to break a law. But his close relationship with you could be perceived as *bending* the law. He collected you from prison, found you a place to live and recommended you to a business acquaintance of his to get you a position with an accountancy firm without revealing your change of name. Then there is Helen Jackson, your cellmate, whose divorce he arranged and whom he later defended unsuccessfully on a murder charge. It was rumoured that Helen was more than just a client to Clive, and with a beautiful woman like you to spice up the story the tabloids will have a field day.'

'I am not news, and Helen is dead. Why would they bother to resurrect old history?' She asked the question but already knew the answer. She saw it in the glint of triumph in his night-black eyes.

'I have connections with the media. I can make sure they do.' He shrugged, as though destroying a man's reputation was nothing to him.

For a moment Beth was speechless and simply stared at him. 'You would actually ruin Clive Hampton, a man respected by all who know him, simply because you think I am a criminal low-life after your brother and his money?'

'I don't have to think. I *know* you are an ex-con, and I *know* you used your considerable charms to get young Bewick under your spell. Now you are doing the same with Tony. He is infatuated by you. As for the money… I can't be certain. But I do know Helen left you a house and a nice chunk of money. Maybe your talent for en-snaring men extends to females too.' He shrugged his shoulders 'Not my business. But Tony is. I stopped you once and I will again.'

He was so wrong that Beth couldn't help but smile. 'You make me sound like the Wicked Witch of the West,' she quipped.

Dante's lips quirked at the corners, but he said nothing. She was too close to what he had been thinking earlier.

Beth wasn't surprised at his lack of response; the man had no sense of humour—although she thought she'd caught the hint of a smile just now. Anyway, what did it matter? Beth had very few options left open to her—if any.

She could tell him the truth about how she had been set up by Timothy Bewick and his partner in crime, James Hudson, and how the pair of them had lied at her trial. But what was the point? She had protested her in-nocence years ago and the jury had found her guilty. Cannavaro had made up his mind about her and noth-ing she said was going to change it now.

'Okay, you win,' Beth conceded. She needed to get away fast, because she was far too aware of him and was watching his lips for a hint of that smile she thought she'd seen… 'Originally I was just going on holiday to Devon, but now I will definitely stay there.'

Beth had often dreamed of living at the coast one day, and after discussing it with Clive it had been an easy decision to make. In the past two weeks plans for the garage conversion had been prepared and submitted to the council, and a contractor had been hired for the refurbishment of the house, but she saw no reason to enlighten Cannavaro. It would feed his monumental ego to let him think she had given in to his demands and he had won.

'I will have to come back for a few days to empty the apartment and retrieve the key Tony keeps for me. Then you and Tony will never see me again. Satisfied?' she demanded caustically.

'No…I would not say that,' Dante drawled softly.

'But you've got what you wanted,' Beth said, confused. Then she saw the way he was looking at her, his eyes roaming over her body with lazy masculine appraisal before moving to her face. His hand on her arm tightened and for a moment she couldn't move, couldn't break away from the eyes holding hers, blatantly showing his sexual desire. Suddenly she was afraid—not of him, but of herself, as the same heated desire held her in thrall and she could no longer ignore the way her body reacted to him.

'Not quite everything… You are an experienced, sophisticated woman and Clive Hampton risked his reputation for the privilege of having you in his bed.'

'That is disgusting. Clive—' Beth cut in, the heat between them instantly turning to anger.

'Don't bother denying it. You still see him and spend the occasional weekend at his home in Richmond. Who knows how many other men enjoy the pleasure of your body?'

Beth stared at him in furious disbelief. 'That is the most despicable, vile lie I have ever heard. I have never slept with Clive. He is a truly honorable man...and you really are a first-class bastard, aren't you?'

Even Dante could see Beth's outrage was genuine and that she was telling the truth—but then he had never really thought Clive was her lover. He had used Clive as a ploy to get his own way, and he felt slightly ashamed, because as well as the anger he also saw the hurt in her emerald eyes.

'Maybe I have been a bit harsh to you, but I am not interested in your other lovers—only Tony.'

Surprised he had actually admitted to being harsh, Beth looked up at him. 'Tony isn't my lover. He is a friend. I do have some,' she said dryly.

'I don't doubt it.' He lifted a finger to stroke her cheek and Beth sucked in a breath, her pulse going haywire. 'You are a lovely woman and even if I believed you and your story that you will stay in Devon, you've said yourself I can't follow you around for the rest of your life. What is to stop you calling Tony? He is my kid brother and, much as I love him, he is far too young to marry but impulsive enough to do just that. I can't take that chance. Which is why I want him to have complete freedom from you.'

At his mention of freedom Beth fought down the urge to scream. *What about my freedom?* The freedom he had taken away so ruthlessly once. She had no doubt that given the chance he would do so again.

As though sensing her frustration he let go of her and stepped back, running a distracted hand through his hair. 'It gives me no pleasure to fight with you, Beth. I know you have succeeded in turning your life around, but you are who you are. Try to see it from my point of view. If you had a young brother who wanted to marry a girl who was a convicted drug dealer, would you be happy about it?' he asked.

Put like that, Beth could see he had a point. 'No, I don't suppose so,' she said. Except in her case she was innocent of any crime.

'You must understand I simply want to protect Tony.' He flopped down on the sofa and glanced up at her. 'And that means getting you out of his life,' he said, a wry smile twisting his lips. 'I flew in from America this morning and have been travelling for hours. Maybe if you made me a coffee it would help me think clearly and hopefully between us we can find a mutual agreeable solution to our problem.'

For a man who did not want to appear harsh, he had an odd way of showing it, Beth thought, but did not say it. 'Fine, I'll make you a coffee. I could use one myself anyway.'

Relieved to escape from his overwhelming presence, she walked out of the room and into the kitchen, taking a few deep breaths to calm her still-racing pulse. Automatically she filled the coffee machine, her head in a whirl. What other kind of solution had he in mind? she wondered. Banishing her to Outer Mongolia, maybe?

She ought to pick up Binkie, walk straight out of the door and go on her way without ever speaking to Cannavaro again. If she only had herself to consider she would. But the thought of Clive stopped her. It was unthinkable that his reputation could be ruined because of her....

Finally Beth decided that all she could do was tell the truth, calmly and succinctly. Maybe Cannavaro would finally listen to her and accept that he had no need to worry about his brother. She would explain again about her friendship with Tony and the non-existent affair, and that she really was moving out anyway. In fact he could check with Steel and White that she had already handed in her notice. Surely that would convince him to believe her, and leave her alone?

Filling two cups with coffee, she placed them on a tray and carried it through to the living room. There was no sign of her guest. Then she heard the sound of curtains being drawn and realised where he was. She exited the room in a rush, to enter the bedroom next door. The curtains were half open and Cannavaro was standing in the bay window.

'What are you doing in here?' Beth demanded. She loved her bedroom and it felt far too intimate, seeing him standing there, all virile male, legs slightly apart, looking out of the window. She had never had a man in her bedroom before, and the picture he presented was very seductive.

It was large room with a high ceiling, and Beth had decorated it in mint green and ivory. The bed was centred on one wall, and on another were wardrobes and her dressing table. Next to the window was her pride and joy: an antique ladies' bureau.

'I am not familiar with this area or the parking.' He turned to look at her. 'So I thought I'd check my car. I only took delivery of it three weeks ago, and I have been abroad for two of them. I wanted to make sure it was okay.' He smiled ruefully. 'I have to confess my secret pleasure is cars. I can't resist buying them and changing them. At the moment I have a dozen, from vintage to the latest model. Ten at home in Italy and two here now.'

He gave her another smile and Beth was surprised that he actually seemed quite human when he was talking about his cars, and not the devil she had thought him.

'I would never have put you down as a petrolhead,' she said. 'You should meet the man who takes care of my car. He is a real fanatic.'

'Your car being the distinctive white one parked outside, I presume?'

'Yes…' Beth was very proud of her car, and had even given it a name. Given what Dante had just told her, his desire to check on his car sounded feasible.

'Very nice…'

He glanced out of the window and then back to her. 'Ah, you have the coffee.' Walking over, he took a cup from the tray and strode back to the window. 'The paintwork on your vehicle is highly original. Come and explain what it represents.'

Beth put the tray down on the dressing table and crossed to the window. Her eyes widened in appreciation at the sleek black Ferrari parked by the side of the road behind her modest Volkswagen, and she could understand perfectly why he was worried about his car. But standing so close to him like this was not a good idea, and she was suddenly very conscious of the close proximity of his body to hers. The quicker she told him about her car, the quicker she would get him out of her bedroom and her apartment. Which was what she wanted, wasn't it?

'The turquoise swirls along the side are meant to

represent the waves of the sea, and if you look really closely you can see the outline of a mermaid and the name "Jess" spelt out by the spray on the crest of a wave. A young man who used to be a graffiti artist with a penchant for stealing cars is now an apprentice mechanic at the local garage. He offered to personalise my car and we chose the design between us.'

'Is his name Jess?' Dante asked, frowning down at her.

'Good heavens, no. Jess was my best friend for a long time, but she's gone now.' As a child Beth had created an imaginary friend called Jess, and such had been her loneliness and desperation in prison she had remembered her again. Suddenly it hit her: how sad for a grown woman to remember such childish things. She sighed. It would seem she would never be truly free of her past.

Dante put the coffee cup down on the windowsill and stepped closer. 'I'm sorry if I have revived sad memories for you, Beth. Contrary to what you think, I do not want to cause you any harm. I simply want you out of Tony's life. He is far too young to be thinking of marriage.'

She looked up into his dark eyes. They were no longer hard and cruel, but gleaming with a warmth that seemed genuine. But she had been fooled by him before, she remembered, and thought again of her decision to explain her situation to him fully.

'From what I know of Tony he is perfectly able to look after himself—though he and Mike do tend to borrow milk, sugar, food…you name it. But, hey, what are friends for?' She shrugged. 'And you are totally wrong. Tony has no desire to marry me or any woman.

He has said so often enough. The only reason he made that comment about wanting to be my fiancé was to get one over on you.'

She looked squarely at him.

'Apparently you are a noted connoisseur of women, and Tony thought that with me on his arm his status would increase a hundred percent in your eyes. It was a joke. He was teasing you because he thinks you are far too serious. In a rash moment I decided to go along with him. Misguidedly, as it has turned out, or you would not be here,' she said wryly. 'And I certainly do not want to marry Tony or any man. I value my independence far too much to risk losing it again. As for money—I have enough of my own, and I really am moving out of here. If you don't believe me you can call Steel and White. They will tell you I resigned five days ago.'

'That won't be necessary, Beth. I believe you. Tony has always been a bit of a joker. You are a beautiful woman. Any man would want you in his bed—I know I would. Two consenting adults...there is nothing wrong with that...but Tony is not like you and I. He is still idealistic enough to equate sex with love. But I realise I may have overdone the protective older brother bit and been a little hard on you.'

Stunned that he believed what she'd said, and even more stunned by his comment that he wanted her and classed her in the 'consenting adults' department, Beth lifted her eyes to his. What she saw in the glittering depths of his eyes made her drag in a trembling breath before continuing. 'That must be a first. You never believed a word I said before.'

'It is not solely a woman's prerogative to change her mind.' He gave her a twisted smile. 'Since meeting you again I've realised I may have misjudged you. I admire the fact you have managed to turn your life around. You are an incredible woman,' he said, and, dipping his head, he brushed her lips with his.

CHAPTER FOUR

BETH STARED AT HIM, her tongue involuntarily tracing her lips, absorbing the taste of him. Heated colour stained her cheeks as she struggled to make sense of her reaction. His kiss had made her forget he was her enemy, the man who had ruined her life.

'You really do believe me?' she murmured.

'I said so. But that does not solve my problem.'

'Problem?' Beth licked her tingling lips; she was losing the plot, she thought. She had told him the truth and he had believed her.

'Don't look at me like that, Beth,' Dante said huskily, having followed the path of her pink tongue as it caressed her lip. 'Just listen to me. There is no need for you to leave your job unless you really want to. I will never say anything to anyone about your name-change or Clive. But I won't be satisfied until you have moved out of this apartment and away from Tony. With that in mind I will find you another apartment. You will not lose out in the monetary sense at all, I can assure you.'

Still struggling to control the trembling his kiss had evoked, it took a long moment for Beth to let the import of his words sink into her fuddled mind. Then she recalled exactly what he had said, and just how clever he was with words, and realised he didn't really believe her at all. Nothing had changed....

As for his offer of an apartment and the mention of money—with his reputation, and given that he'd said he wanted her and had kissed her—she had to wonder if he expected her to come with the apartment too....

Beth glanced up at him, big and strong—all raw sexuality—and wondered whether she would be that averse to the idea if he *did* mean it. If she was brutally honest, she had to admit that she probably wouldn't be. She was still hot from his kiss, and looking at him simply increased the heat... But she was not cut out to be any man's mistress. She had suffered more than most for her freedom, and she was never giving it up again for anyone.

She could not help thinking that Dante Cannavaro had haunted her dreams for long enough. But he thought her guilty of just about every sin in the book, and maybe at twenty-seven it was finally time she tasted those sins. And who better to do it with than the man before her? Exorcise him from her head, her life, for good...?

At least it would show him that she wasn't the *femme fatale* he had accused her of being, with a string of lovers in her wake. It might even do him some good—show him he wasn't infallible—and maybe he would not be so quick to judge others, she reasoned. Though, being honest, she knew it wasn't just reason driving her. She wanted him in a physical way she had never felt for any man in her life.

'That's an idea,' she said slowly, her mind made up. She never flirted with men, but there was always a first time for everything. She half closed her eyes to shut out the disturbing darkness of his handsome face, then, drawing in a shaky breath, deliberately glanced up at him through the thick veil of her lashes and ran the tip of her tongue over her lips. 'I will certainly consider it.' She saw his eyes glitter with triumph before darkening with a different emotion that brought an answering response in hers.

'Good,' he growled as his hand snaked round her waist, his long fingers splaying across the naked band of skin. She shivered at his touch. 'I knew you would see sense, Beth.' And as he spoke the last word he pulled her gently against his long body and brought his mouth down on hers again.

This wasn't sense, Beth thought, and panicked for a second. But with the lazy heat of the summer afternoon filling the shadowed confines of her bedroom her pulse quickened and her body turned hot and sensitive beneath her clothes. Willingly her lips parted to the slow penetration of his tongue, stroking and exciting all her senses. She ignored the voice in her head that tried to warn her that this was wrong on so many levels. Her slender body melted against him, the long, passionate, drugging kiss driving every sane thought from her head.

Her eyes were tightly shut, and she was conscious of the swelling fullness of her breasts against his broad chest and the damp moistness between her thighs. She was floating blindly on a sea of erotic sensations she had never knew existed before. Involuntarily her hands grasped his arms. She could feel his body heat through the fine silk of his shirt as her fingers traced the contours of muscular biceps and moved up to curve over his broad shoulders. She had felt an instant affinity with Dante the very first time she had seen him and had never understood why, but now she did—with every atom of her being.

When he pulled his head back she was clinging to him, her hands tight against his neck, her face uplifted. Her emerald eyes slowly opened and her soft lips parted, swollen with passion.

'*Dio*! You are beautiful,' he groaned, one hand lifting to sweep a few strands of her hair from her brow. Long fingers stroked the delicate arch of one eyebrow and the curve of her cheek before finally moving to the outline of her lush lips. 'So beautiful,' he repeated, his head lowering.

His kiss and the almost feverish movements of his hand on her back, her hips, and down her thighs to her bare legs, sent a white-hot flame of passion through her, consuming them both. Her lips clung hungrily to his, her hands stealing up his neck until they buried themselves in his black hair, twining among the thick strands.

Without removing his lips from hers he lifted her and carried her to the bed. Lowering her onto it, he slid down beside her. She felt the pressure of his great body against her, his kiss burning her lips as though he could not bring himself to stop.

'Wait...' Beth murmured against his mouth, her heart thudding like a jackhammer. The sensations he was arousing were so overwhelming she was having second thoughts—but not for long. Her body seemed to have a will of its own and she was aching for more.

'Why wait?' Dante said hoarsely, lifting his head to stare down at her. 'I've wanted you from the moment I saw you and I believe you feel the same.' His eyes burned black. 'Tell me it is so.'

She saw the dark stain of desire in his face and knew it was reflected in her own as he shrugged off his shirt. She felt her throat tighten, and knew she could not deny him—didn't want to. 'Oh, yes…' she said breathlessly, totally enthralled by the sight of his broad muscular chest, the golden skin and the light tracing of black curling body hair. Eagerly, like a child, she reached out to touch him, her fingers stroking over his chest in a caress.

He reared back. 'In a moment you can touch me everywhere,' he said huskily, and reached for her.

With the deftness of long experience he removed her clothes, and the rest of his, and leant over her.

She had never seen a totally naked man in the flesh before, and Dante was magnificent—from his broad shoulders down over his flat stomach. Her eyes widened at his powerful erection; it was vaguely frightening, but fascinating, and she was totally mesmerised by the beauty of his big golden body. Beth didn't have time to be embarrassed by her own nudity or the aroused male scent of him. The hard-packed muscular length of him was a potent aphrodisiac and excitement exploded inside her. *So this is what sex is about,* she thought, and then stopped thinking altogether.

His lips and hands were all over her, touching her, kissing her throat and her shoulders. His fingers caressed her and the incredible sensations searing through her obliterated everything except this moment. His mouth found her breasts, and the hot, seductive suckling and nipping went on and on until she was mindless, her hand grasping the back of his head to hold him there.

He moved to kiss her mouth again and their tongues duelled in the thrust and parry of passion. She reached around his broad back, her slender fingers stroking over his satin-smooth skin, her fingertips tracing the length of his spine before trailing over the hard curve of his buttocks. She trembled as he leant back and stared down at her with molten black eyes, his strong hands shaping her breasts, the indentation of her waist and her hips, before parting her legs.

'You *are* a redhead,' he said huskily, his palm cupping her feminine mound.

She gasped as his long fingers delved into the hot, wet warmth, a finger pressing on the nub of feminine nerves, and she shuddered uncontrollably.

'You like that,' Dante growled, his eyes burning into hers, and he bent his head to lick the tip of one breast while his fingers continued their skilful torment.

She could not speak, she could barely breathe as a sensual storm spread like wildfire to the core of her. She reached out to him, her hand roaming over his massive chest, her nails grazing a hard male nipple, and felt him shudder. Her hand slid lower to his rock-hard erection, touching and exploring him intimately. She wanted him with a passion and a hunger she had never felt before in her life.

His breath caught audibly in the back of his throat. 'Beth...' he growled, and grasped her wrist to pin her hand to the bed. 'You are sure you want this?' He lowered his dark head and kissed her breasts and her mouth again, whispering her name between kisses while his fingers renewed their torment at the very centre of her femininity, driving her into a vortex of sensual pleasure she had never even imagined existed.

'Yes,' Beth whimpered, as her body bucked and writhed beneath him. The incredible seductiveness of his mouth and his hands and the heat of his powerful body, sweat-slicked and taut against her flesh, was driving her insane. Frantically she ran her hands over his shoulders, her nails digging into his broad back, lost to everything but Dante.

He eased back her thighs and rose over her. He was there, where she ached with need for him, probing gently, then thrusting harder, and suddenly her body tensed, torn by a sharp pain.

He stopped, staring down at her with shock widening his smouldering black eyes. 'No!' he growled, his face taut with passion.

Instinctively she locked her long legs around his waist and with a low groan he moved again slightly, slowly stretching her to accept him. Miraculously the pain was gone, replaced with unimaginable pleasure as he gradually thrust deeper and deeper.

His heart thudded against her as she felt the exquisite tension tighten and grow, until she thought she could not bear it any more, and finally she fell shuddering into a kaleidoscopic world of a myriad sensations and ultimate satisfaction, taking him with her.

Eyes closed, Beth was conscious of every muscle, sinew and nerve of her body in a new way—a wonderful, awesome way that there were no words invented to explain. Euphoric and completely at one with Dante, she relished his heavy naked body over hers, his head resting on her shoulder, the rasping sound of his breath and the thundering beat of his heart against hers gradually slowing.

When he moved to roll onto his back Beth opened her eyes to see him lean up on one elbow and look down at her. Her lips parted in a wide smile, her green eyes shining like emeralds in her flushed face.

'Beth—Jane—whatever your name is, you are an exquisitely desirable woman and one hell of a surprise,' he said, but did not smile back.

Beth's smile faded a little as she stared at his hard, handsome face, not sure if he meant that as a compliment. He was frowning, and she saw the glint of anger in his night-black eyes. Why was he angry?

'Dante?' She said his name questioningly.

'Finally you say my name. It comes a little late after what we have just done, don't you think?'

Beth heard the hint of mockery in his tone and was chilled by it—but then what had she expected? Avowals of love? Never in a million years. With her euphoria fading fast, she came back to reality. At the barbecue he had told her they had a mutual sexual attraction but that it could not be acted upon.

Now he was no longer engaged and that was no longer the case. It was sex—just sex. Something he engaged in on a regular basis with a variety of women. The fact it was new to Beth meant nothing. It was still just sex. The reason she was here now was to get him out of her head once and for all. Not the best idea she had ever had, but she had proved a point.

'You know what they say—better late than never,' she forced herself to say lightly. 'And after this I don't think I'll have to say your name much more.' With her body still throbbing, she put on the act of her life. 'Your problem is solved. Now you know you were wrong about me. I have never had sex with Tony or any man.' Rolling away from him, she slid her legs over the side of the bed and stood up. She glanced down at him to add, 'And after this I probably never will again—once was enough.'

Unconscious of her naked state, she gathered up her clothes and put them back on without looking at Dante again.

The silence between them was interrupted by the doorbell ringing.

'Don't answer,' Dante commanded.

Beth ignored him and, slipping her feet into her sandals, ran her hands through her hair to sweep it back behind her ears as she walked out of the bedroom. It would probably be a salesman, she thought. But she found that she was wrong. Before she got to the front door she heard a key turn in the lock and Tony walked in.

'Beth—I thought you would be long gone by now. I saw your car outside and wondered what had happened to you.'

'I got delayed by Binkie,' she replied, and conveniently the cat chose that moment to stroll into the hall and wrap himself around her ankles. 'Then I had an unexpected—'

But her weak explanation was cut off by another voice.

'Tony—nice to see you. I wondered when you'd be back.'

Beth tensed and glanced back, to see Dante leaning casually against the doorjamb of the bedroom wearing his trousers with his shirt half buttoned and his black hair curling damply on his broad brow. She cringed with embarrassment.

'Dante!' Tony frowned. 'What are you doing here?'

'I called to see you to show you my new Ferrari and knocked on the wrong front door. Beth answered and we had a coffee and a chat.' He nodded towards the bedroom. 'I was just looking through the front window to check my car was still there.'

Beth was surprised at his glib answer, but also relieved.

'Oh, yes!' Tony drawled. 'I saw the car. It's in my usual parking spot.' His blue eyes flicked suspiciously between Beth and Dante, and finally settled on Beth. 'Is he right, Beth? I thought you were leaving at one? It's five o'clock now. That is a heck of a lot of cups of coffee.'

Bending down, Beth picked up Binkie and hugged him to her chest, her mind spinning. The truth was always the best option—or some of it, she decided. 'I was supposed to be leaving at one, but it was after three before I managed to get Binkie in his carrier for the third time. The doorbell rang and I forgot to fasten it before I answered the door. Dante came in, tripped over the carrier, and Binkie shot out again—causing Dante to stumble and fall flat on the floor. It was quite a crash. He is a big man.'

She saw Tony smile.

'You fell over her cat?'

'Yes,' Dante said dryly, not in the least amused.

'Now, *that* I would have liked to have seen.' Tony chuckled. 'I'm surprised Beth didn't kick you out there and then for harming Binkie. She loves that cat.'

'Tony! Poor Dante was really winded,' Beth chipped in. 'Though I did consider it.' It gave her some satisfaction to see Dante discomfited for a change.

'Well, it's not surprising he was winded. He *is* a lot older than you and I, Beth.'

Beth saw the sparkle of devilment in Tony's eyes

and smiled at his quip about his brother's age. It was either that or cry—and Cannavaro had caused enough tears in her life already. She wasn't about to shed a single one more.

'True...' she said, holding the smile. 'But I have been delayed long enough. If I want to get there by dark you two will have to go now. I'm going to put Binkie into his carrier and we can finally leave.'

'Okay,' Tony agreed, then added, 'I can see you are in a hurry, and I can only apologise for my brother delaying you.' He grinned at her. 'Shall I still check on your apartment until you get back?'

'Yes, of course.' Beth couldn't help smiling. Tony was an incorrigible but very likable young man—the exact opposite of his hard-faced, cynically arrogant brother... She realised she was going to miss Tony and Mike. Their happy-go-lucky attitude to life had been a tonic for her. But it was for the best that she was leaving.

'You heard, bro. Beth wants us out—and in case you've forgotten I'll see you later at the parents' anniversary party.' He turned towards the door, and then turned back. 'Oh, by the way, Dante—don't forget your shoes. The barefoot look really doesn't suit you....' he said, and walked out.

'So once was enough, hmm?' Dante drawled as the front door shut.

Still holding the cat, Beth stared at Dante as though she had never seen him before. 'More than enough,' she intoned icily.

'If you had told me I was your first I would have been more careful.'

'You've got to be joking. You never believe a word I say—though you pretend to when it suits you.'

'Maybe. But I'm curious, Beth. Why did you hang on to your virginity for so long? No, don't bother answering. I know…' he said without pause. 'You told me Tony was just teasing when he said he wanted you to be his fiancée, but I think it was you that was doing the teasing. That is how you operate. You get pleasure from leading young men on and denying them what they want until they're crazy about you and will do anything you say. First Timothy Bewick and now Tony. There have probably been many more,' he declared cynically.

He could not have said anything more likely to enrage Beth and, putting Binkie down, she moved towards him, her anger so livid her cheeks were scarlet with it. She registered the arrogant stance of his big body, his hands tucked easily into the pockets of his trousers. He appeared every inch the sophisticated lawyer, with his confident summing-up of the situation, and it was not surprising the jury in her case had believed every word he said.

Even half dressed he exuded an aura of power, conviction and a sheer masculine magnetism that was almost impossible to ignore. It was inherent in his every move, every gesture, but this time Beth was immune to his lethal appeal. She fought down the urge to rant and rave at him and instead stopped a few inches in front of him, deliberately raising her gaze to his hard face, her green eyes contemptuous.

'No. But if that is what you want to think to salve your conscience, be my guest. We both know that at my trial, when you painted me as some *femme fatale* who slept with young men to control them, the real liar was you.' She dropped each word slowly and precisely into the tense silence. 'You try living with that, as I have for the last eight years. You might actually discover a conscience, though I doubt it. Your sort never does.' Disgust was evident in her tone. 'As for Tony—you saw for yourself we are just good friends. But then I doubt a man like you *has* any friends.'

Dante shrugged and, taking his hand from the pocket of his pants, ran one long finger down her burning cheek to tilt her chin up and study her flushed and furious face.

'You are overwrought, and in a way I don't blame you. I am much older, more experienced than the boys you usually play with, and you got more than you bargained for. But you were with me all the way, so don't try to pretend otherwise. You are only fooling yourself. I have never known a more eager lover. And I did not lie in court. As a lawyer I simply implied—there is a difference.'

Beth shook her head, unable to deny what he said, and stepped away from him. 'Yes, you are right, of course. The difference in my case was freedom or a three-year sentence,' she said caustically. 'Now, if that is all, for about the tenth time of asking, will you get out of here? I never want to see you again.'

'The feeling is mutual. You can rest assured I will never be back.'

'At last a mutually acceptable solution. We have a deal. We will stay far away from each other—a continent would be good,' she sniped, and walked into the kitchen, battling to contain the pain and anger he had revived in her.

She hated him, and she must never forget it again. She had heard it said that love and hate were different sides of the same coin, but she could not let herself think that way—could not let herself think of the pleasure his body had given her. It was just sex, she told herself again, and her overreaction was probably because she had waited so long to experience it.

Dante resisted the urge to follow Beth. Finding his shoes, he put them on and returned to the living room to retrieve his jacket. He had done what he'd set out to do. Beth was moving out, Tony would be free of her influence and that was what Dante had wanted... So why did he feel like the lowest of the low? Probably because Beth had hit a nerve with her crack about his performance in court. She had done him no favours with her crack about his performance in bed, either....

Oddly, he felt guilty on both counts...and it was not an emotion he was familiar with. But then he was not a man prone to emotions of any sort. It would pass.

Dante got in his car and drove away without a backward glance. Beth was a stunning woman, but not for him. She was not wife material, and she was far too dangerous to his peace of mind to be his mistress.

Although in a way he could not help admiring her. She had managed to change her life very successfully and perfectly legally, he thought as he skilfully manoeuvred the car through the rush-hour traffic. Jane—or Beth—or whatever her real name was had grown into one beautiful, intelligent, feisty woman whom he suspected could hold her own with either man or woman. She had certainly given as good as she'd got from *him*.

He was still smarting from her *once was enough* comment—not that he believed her. Beth was the most naturally sensual woman he had ever met, and had reacted to his lightest touch and caress. She had instinctively known how to return the pleasure too. She had been fire and light in his arms, eager to take everything he could give her, and he could still feel the sting of her nails on his back. He couldn't remember ever having lost control with a lover the way he had with Beth, and the scent and feel of her luscious body beneath him had blown his mind. His body stirred again now at the thought of her.

Suddenly another thought hit him like a thunderbolt. He had forgotten protection. How could he have been so careless?

And in the next second Dante Cannavaro did the unthinkable—for him—and compounded his carelessness by rear-ending the pickup truck in front of him, having not noticed the traffic had stopped for a red light.

He reversed out from under the flatbed of the truck— to the further detriment of his Ferrari—and pulled up to exchange details with the driver of the pickup. Dante loved his cars, and he had never so much as dented one in his life until he'd met Beth Lazenby. Maybe she was a witch and had put a hex on him, he thought, stifling a groan as he surveyed the battered bonnet of his new Ferrari.

He debated going back to tell Beth about his mistake in forgetting to use protection, then, coming to his senses, thought better of it. Given the type of woman he knew Beth to be, he was pretty sure that if his mistake resulted in a pregnancy she would contact him with dollar signs in her eyes.

CHAPTER FIVE

BETH OPENED HER EYES to see the early-morning rays of the sun flooding the bedroom and stretched lazily. She looked across at the large windows that folded back to open almost the whole room to the balcony and the sea beyond and sighed contentedly. She loved this house, she thought, a soft smile curling her lips as she glanced around the master bedroom.

The cream-and-blue flower-sprigged wallpaper with matching curtains and bedlinen were a little faded now, as the master suite with bathroom and dressing room had been refurbished to Helen's taste when she had been released from prison. Beth never wanted to change it as the room reminded her of her friend and gave her a feeling of serenity. It was her safe haven from the rest of the world.

A builder and decorator had completed the refurbishment of the rest of the house last week. The other three bedrooms on this floor had en-suite bathrooms now, plus the two bedrooms on the top floor. The house had never looked better, and the rental potential had increased significantly. Beth was quite happy with what she had achieved.

Sliding her legs over the side of the bed, she stood

up and walked into the dressing room, collecting briefs and an exotically printed slip dress, and then entered the bathroom.

Yesterday she had received notice that her plans to convert the roof space of the garage into a two-bedroomed apartment had been passed. The builder was due to start in three weeks' time.

With a sense of satisfaction she stepped into the shower and turned on the water. She had slept without dreaming of Dante Cannavaro or thinking of him the minute she woke up for a couple of weeks now, and her plan to exorcise him from her mind by having sex with him seemed to be working.

She had definitely made the right decision. She loved her new life—the freedom to work when she wanted to or walk out of the door and breathe the fresh sea air or take a swim and go surfing if the mood struck her. She had even acquired a slight tan, and for the first time in ages no longer felt she had to be careful or fearful of the past coming back to haunt her. She was her own woman, mistress of her own destiny, and Cannavaro had been shoved back into the box he had occupied for the last few years and was not worth thinking about.

She slipped on her briefs and dress and ran a brush through the tangled mass of her hair. Down here she never bothered with a hairdryer or the electric straightening tongs that had been a part of her daily routine in London in order to present a sleek, professional image. Much as she had liked her old job, Beth had not really enjoyed living in London. But she had fulfilled Helen's wish and become a success. Now she was out of the rat race and hoping to be equally as successful in her new venture.

She had certainly made a good start, she thought happily. She already had a few bookings for next year, by which time the garage apartment would certainly be ready. She would have to work two days a week in the house when it was rented out, but that was no problem—and much preferable to working all week in an office.

An hour later, having fed Binkie and with a cup of tea and two slices of French toast in her tummy, Beth was ready to face the day. Janet was coming over at two with her daughter, and they were driving into town to shop before returning to the house for dinner.

Janet's father had been employed on a part-time basis here for years, as gardener and caretaker, and Beth had met Janet the first time she'd visited. Now she considered her a friend. Janet had married young and had a four-year-old daughter called Annie. Tragically, her soldier husband had been killed in Afghanistan last year, and after his death Janet was back living with her parents. Sometimes Janet and Annie stayed with Beth for a night or two, and it suited them both.

Carrying her second cup of tea and her sunglasses, Beth opened the front door onto the long terrace that ran the length of the cottage, with steps down to the garden path and the road, with the beach and sea beyond. She sat down on one of the eight captain's chairs and looked out over the bay. The sea was as calm as a millpond.

Blinded by the glare of the sun on the water for a moment, she blinked and put on her sunglasses—then blinked again as the roar of a car split the silence.

A big black Bentley...

She watched as the luxury car stopped in front of her gate and with a sinking heart recognised the driver as he opened the door and got out. Her heart sank further at the sight of Dante Cannavaro, standing surveying the bay.

His black hair gleamed like polished jet in the sunlight. Aviator sunglasses hid his eyes, but nothing could detract from the golden chiselled perfection of his features. His great body was clad in a black polo shirt open at the neck, and hip-hugging black jeans that clung to his muscular thighs and long legs like a second skin. He was strikingly attractive. Simply looking at the man was enough to make most women go weak at the knees.

Beth was glad she was sitting down, because her plan to rid him from her mind—which only earlier she had thought was working—had obviously not worked after all. Why, oh, why, she wondered despairingly, after twenty-seven years of hardly being aware of the sexual side of her nature, had she only got to *see* Dante Cannavaro for her pulse to race and her temperature to soar?

Filled with self-loathing at her reaction, she lifted her cup and took a drink of tea, trying to ignore him. She did not know what had brought him here and she was not going to ask. He certainly wasn't a typical daytripper. As a super-rich, sophisticated international lawyer, a luxury resort somewhere exotic was surely more his style.

Looking around, Dante was surprised by the beauty of the cove—and more so by the house. He had pictured some quaint old cottage as he had driven over the headland and down the cliff road to the harbour. He had called at the local pub to ask directions to the cottage of Miss Lazenby, and had been treated to a glowing tribute to Beth by the landlord. He had also been

JACQUELINE BAIRD 85

informed that the cottage was the best holiday rental for miles around, and a great little earner for Beth, and then told how to find the place. Dante had driven to almost the opposite end of the bay, as per instructions, and had been surprised.

The 'cottage' was a large white-rendered double-fronted house, with a wide terrace that ran the width of the building. Another balcony ran the length of the first floor, and in the roof was a third, complete with a flagpole and a telescope fixed to the glass guard-rail. All the windows were virtually walls of glass that opened onto the respective terraces. It was in a magnificent position, looking straight out to sea, and set in about an acre of garden with a stone wall surrounding it. The road that ran between the house and the beach came to a dead end a few hundred yards farther on at the foot of the cliffs in a small car park.

Turning, Dante shook his head in amazement. Somehow he could not see the elegant redhead, the professional big-city accountant, settling down in a place that looked as if time had forgotten it. But then he had trouble seeing Beth as anything but naked beneath him, and knowing the mistake he had made was driving him crazy.

As for Faith Cove—if it had more than a thousand residents he'd be surprised.

Carved in the stone column of the house's entrance gate was 'The Sail Loft' and, appropriately, a sailing dinghy was parked on the hard standing to one side of the house. A rack for surfboards with two in evidence stood beside it. On the other side was a long drive that led to a large garage at the rear of the property. The doors were open and her very distinctive Volkswagen was visible.

He was impressed. The land alone, situated as it was with spectacular views of the bay, had to be worth a good deal of money, Dante realised, never mind the house.

He tensed as he caught sight of Beth, sitting on the terrace, and surprisingly felt a moment of doubt. Ironically, he had arranged his schedule to have the month of September free to get married. Instead he had spent the first few days catching up on estate business and then supposedly relaxing. His housekeeper, Sophie, had made relaxing difficult, though. She was another woman who had already 'bought the hat' for the wedding that never was, and she'd spent most of her time giving him dire warnings that if he didn't marry soon he would be lucky to see his children grow up. It was hard to argue with a woman who had changed his nappy as a child, and finally he had given up and gone to Rome where he'd accepted a new case. He'd had a couple of dinner dates with an old flame, determined to get on with his life, but it hadn't helped....

Far from forgetting Beth Lazenby, as he'd intended, he had found she'd occupied his thoughts for the last eight weeks to the point of distracting him from his work—not something that had ever happened to him before. Women had their place in his life—usually his bed. But never in his head...

He had reread the investigator's report on Beth and realised that Jane Mason had lost her parents only twelve months before her trial. He was surprised that her lawyer, Miss Sims, had not brought that fact up in court. Any good defence lawyer would have used the death of her parents as part of a character profile—troubled young lady who had lost her parents recently....

But then Miss Sims had not been a good lawyer. She had barely challenged anything he had said, and had stopped him on the way out to congratulate him, he recalled. Suddenly Dante found himself making excuses for Beth. Had he been too harsh with her? Alone in the world, she might easily have gone off the rails with grief... Not that it mattered. The evidence had been solid and the jury had found her guilty, he reminded himself. But he was a man always supremely confident in his decisions and he never second-guessed himself. The fact that Beth was making him do just that shocked him rigid. It had to stop.

Finally, yesterday morning, after a frustrating weekend, he had rationalised that there was nothing to be gained by waiting with the sword of Damocles hanging over his head. He needed to make sure Beth was definitely not pregnant before he got involved with another woman. His legal team could take care of work. His presence wasn't essential until a client meeting on Wednesday.

His decision made, he'd taken a flight to London. He'd called Tony, pretty sure he would know where Beth was, but had got no reply. Then he'd called at her old apartment on the off-chance that she had lied about everything and was still living there. Only to be faced by a young man who said he had no idea where the last tenant had gone.

Finally he'd caught up with Tony late afternoon and discovered Beth had been gone for weeks and had set up in business for herself. But as her loyal friend Tony had refused to give Dante her phone number or her address at Beth's specific request.

After checking the investigator's report again he had found the address of her cottage and set off at the crack of dawn to drive here, confront her, and dismiss doubt and the woman from his life once and for all and get back to normal.

At least that was what he'd told himself. But now, as he looked at her exquisite profile and the contrast of her red hair against the ever-so-slightly sun-kissed skin of her bare shoulders, a basic, more earthy desire began to heat his blood.

Beth heard the click of the gate and glanced down to see Dante stalk up the path and leap up the steps to come and stand towering over her. He became a big black shadow against the sun and memories of the past came rushing back. Involuntarily she shivered. Whether it was because of the old dreams or the sex or both, she wasn't sure. All she was sure of was that his physical presence disturbed her far too much for her peace of mind.

'Good morning, Beth. Lovely place you have here—though a little hard to find. I've been driving since six and could join you in a cup of coffee,' he declared, glancing at the cup in her hand as he sank down onto another captain's chair.

'It's not coffee, it's tea. And if you go back the way you came there is a small café next to the shop on the harbour. Try there,' Beth suggested bluntly. Dante Cannavaro had said he would leave her alone. He had some nerve, turning up here.

'Oh, come on, Beth. That's not very hospitable after

all we have been to each other....' he drawled, and removed his sunglasses.

She saw humour in his dark eyes, and more as he let his gaze roam over her, lingering on the swell of her breasts beneath the cotton of her dress with undisguised male lust.

'No way,' she snapped, feeling uncomfortably warm. 'You agreed we would never meet again. I've kept my side of the deal, so what's your excuse for turning up here and breaking it?' she demanded.

'Extenuating circumstances—and strictly speaking you're wrong. I never actually agreed to stay out of your life, only never to reveal...' He paused, then continued, 'My inside knowledge of you.'

Beth felt her eyes widen and the colour rise in her face at his choice of words, as she was sure he had meant it to. Without thought, she swung her hand in a swift arc to slap his face, but he caught her wrist.

'Now, Beth, that is no way to greet an old friend,' he drawled in a deadly low tone, and lowered her arm down to her thigh.

She tugged her wrist free but had more sense than to try to hit him again.

'I had a pretty tough job finding you again.'

'You shouldn't have bothered. You are not welcome here,' Beth said bluntly. Leaning forward, before she could stop him, he flicked off her sunglasses and his dark eyes clashed with her angry green.

'That's better, Beth. I want to see your reaction when I tell you the reason I am here.'

Beth went very still, her face expressionless, when really she was so mad she wanted to throttle him. But she realised his being here and his last comment sounded like a threat. She looked out to sea for a long moment to regain her composure and reviewed every one of her past encounters with him in her mind. She came to a conclusion. She slowly turned her head to glance up at his harsh, handsome features through the fine curtain of her lashes.

'There is nothing that you can do or say to me that is worse than you have done already,' she said with deliberate softness.

Amazingly, dark colour washed up his face and he drew back, his mouth twisting. 'I sincerely hope not,' he said cryptically, a frown creasing his broad brow.

Beth had the odd notion he was not only embarrassed, but worried.

'But get me a coffee and I will tell you.'

His tone was hard and demanding again, and it set Beth's teeth on edge. For a moment there she had begun to think that Dante was almost human. Big mistake... and not one she intended to repeat.

'No,' she said defiantly. 'I remember what happened the last time you demanded coffee....' She glanced up and caught the gleam of desire in his dark eyes that the memory of their last meeting had evoked and felt an answering surge of heat spread through her body. Stupid thing to say.... She lowered her eyes to try to gather her wits. But focusing on the open neck of his polo shirt was not helping her....

'I did not invite you here, but obviously your investigator informed you I own this place,' she said in a voice that was not quite steady. She ploughed on regardless. 'I do not want you here. I have absolutely no interest in a single word you say. Is that clear enough for you?'

'Yes, but it might be difficult,' Dante said, looking down at Beth.

He felt a strange tightening in his chest as he did so. It was incredible how young, how innocent she looked, with her hair washed and left to dry in surprisingly silken waves. She wore no make-up, and was wearing a simple, brightly patterned summer dress that skimmed over her breasts and slender body. He noticed she wasn't wearing a bra and stiffened, remembering the full firmness of her breasts and the erotic taste of her nipples in his mouth. He also remembered that thanks to him she was not physically innocent anymore—and, of course, the real reason he was here.

His mouth tightened grimly. He was angry for letting her obvious attributes get to him and, straightening up, dismissed the wayward thoughts from his mind, determined to get this over with quickly.

'Look at me, Beth,' he demanded, and watched her raise her head, her expression guarded. 'This is a serious matter. Are you on the pill?'

'No, of course not,' she said without thinking.

'In that case we might have a problem. It may have escaped your attention, but I did not use protection when we had sex. You could be pregnant, and if you are I need to make suitable arrangements.'

'What?' Beth cried, appalled, as the true reason for Dante being here registered in her mind. It had never occurred to her that she might get pregnant—how stupid was that? Would she never learn? Was she sentenced to go through life being made a fool of by this man? she wondered. 'You didn't use…?' Of course he hadn't. She hadn't noticed, but he had just said so, and she suddenly had a hysterical desire to laugh.

'No. It was my fault and I take full responsibility. I am prepared to take care of everything, all the monetary aspects, should the worst circumstance arise.'

'You are unbelievable! You sound like a lawyer even when you drop a bombshell like that on me!' Beth exclaimed, thinking the only thing that would be arising was her stomach if his suspicion was true. Because no way would she take a penny from Dante Cannavaro under *any* circumstance.

'What can I say? I am what I am?' He shrugged negligently.

Ignoring him, Beth swiftly thought back over the eight weeks she had been here and realised she had been so busy planning and working she hadn't noticed she had missed her period. Suddenly Dante's fear was a very real possibility. Her recent aversion to coffee, which Janet had remarked on when Beth had switched to drinking tea, now held a different connotation. But she hadn't been sick—well, not physically. Though she *had* felt nauseous and had blamed it on the pervasive smell of the decorator's paint that had filled the house for weeks.

The little colour she had leached from her face. The very idea filled her with horror; not the thought of a baby—she would love to have a child of her own, someone to love unconditionally—but with Dante Cannavaro as its father! To be connected to him for years by a child didn't bear thinking about....

Then another even more disturbing thought occurred to Beth. What exactly was he offering to pay for—take care of?

She looked at him with dislike. 'By "monetary aspects" do you mean you will pay for an abortion if I am pregnant?' she asked.

'Is that what you want?' he prompted, his hard face expressionless.

'No, never,' she said instinctively.

'Good, because if that *was* what you wanted I would have done everything in my power to convince you otherwise. So, are you pregnant or not?'

She turned her head to stare out to sea again, suddenly very afraid. Dante was a powerful, clever man, and very persuasive—as she knew to her cost. If she *was* pregnant, and if she had a healthy baby and he decided to claim custody, where would that leave her? She was probably worrying unnecessarily, but Dante was a lawyer, and she had no doubt he was ruthless enough to use her past history against her in court. What chance would she have of keeping the baby herself?

Beth looked back at Dante and considered lying. She had loved her adoptive parents, and had no idea who her biological parents were. All she knew was that as a baby she had been left in a sports bag in the emergency department of a hospital. Her mother had never been found. With her own lack of a true identity she knew instinctively that there was no way she could refuse her own child the right to know its father.

'I don't know. It's too early to tell,' she said calmly. It wasn't really a lie, there could be other reasons why she was late, but offhand she could not think of one.

'Don't be ridiculous.'

He rose to his full intimidating height and Beth swallowed hard.

'You are an intelligent, adult woman—you must know if you have missed menstruating.'

'I am not the ridiculous one here,' she shot back. 'I have some excuse, but for a man of your age and experience to forget protection is ridiculous.'

'Point taken.' Dante grimaced. 'But you still have not answered my question. Have you missed your period?'

'Maybe. I don't know. I'm not regular anyway,' Beth said, and immediately wished she had told an outright lie. But she had been so shocked at the thought of pregnancy, and Dante had been so blunt, she had not had time to think things through properly and had simply reacted.

'I don't have patience and I am a busy man. I need to know now, so I can rearrange my schedule if I have to without too much inconvenience. I have a meeting in Rome at midday tomorrow as it is. When I arrived in London yesterday I expected to find you there—not miles away in the middle of nowhere. You said there was a café? Come, I need a coffee.' He reached out a hand. 'And if there is a pharmacy we can get a pregnancy test at the same time and settle the matter now.'

Beth's mouth fell open. 'Are you crazy? I could never buy a pregnancy test in the chemist here. Everyone knows me and it would be around the village in a flash.'

'So we will go to the nearest town.'

Beth tried to argue with him. What man in his right mind went looking for a woman after what had been basically a one-night stand and demanded a pregnancy test? The nearest town was a forty-minute drive away, and she was going there this afternoon with her friend Janet and her daughter anyway. She would get one then.

But he was not prepared to wait. Nothing she said would deter him, and ten minutes later she was sitting in his car.

Silently seething in the passenger seat, Beth watched as he walked around the bonnet and slid into the driving seat. She caught the male scent of his aftershave as he closed the door, saw his chiselled profile, the slight darkening of his firm jawline and the sensuous mouth. Hastily she dropped her gaze, but the denim pulled tight across his thigh so close to hers was no help. Everything about him was so masculine... Her heart skipped a beat and it was hard to breathe. He affected her senses in every way, and yet he was the last man on earth she should be attracted to.

'Nice car. What happened to your Ferrari? Tired of it already?' Beth asked snidely. Anything to take her mind off the sheer physicality of the man and her own troubled thoughts.

'*You* happened,' Dante shot back.

'What do you mean, I happened?' Beth queried.

He turned in his seat to look at her, a rueful smile twisting his lips. 'After I left your apartment I was driving back to my place when it suddenly struck me what I had done—or, more precisely, *not* done. It was just as big a shock to me then as it was to you today, and for the first time in my life I ran into the back of a truck at a red light and buckled the front of my car.'

'You hit a truck?' Beth exclaimed, her green eyes sparkling with amusement. 'With your new Ferrari?' She knew that Dante loved his cars, and it gave her great pleasure to realise he was just as likely as the next man to crash his car.

'It is back in the factory in Italy being repaired—which is why I am driving the Bentley. I was in America until ten days ago, and I meant to pick it up when I got back to Italy. I never got time.'

'You seem to have plenty of time to come here,' she said flatly.

'Yes—but only because I made a mistake with you. I do not like indecision of any kind and I am not pre-pared to wait any longer. It is essential that I know if you are pregnant. If you are I will need to make some readjustments to my life and so will you. We are in this together, Beth, whether we like it or not.'

Dante had ended on a serious note, and Beth looked away as he started the engine and they moved off.

He was right, she thought fatalistically. Better to find out now. Though in her heart of hearts she had a growing conviction that she was. If the pregnancy was confirmed she was going to have to deal with Dante Cannavaro…and, given her past experience with the man, the thought did not fill her with confidence….

CHAPTER SIX

Two hours later a very subdued Beth got out of the car in front of her house, still mortified by the way Dante had behaved at the chemist. He'd had no shame, demanding to know from the female assistant which was the most reliable pregnancy test while Beth had stood embarrassed by his side, wishing the ground would open and swallow her up—or preferably Dante...

Now, after so long in his company, her nerves were stretched to breaking point and the thought of what lay ahead added to her stress levels. Her happy mood on waking up was long gone....

'Let's go inside and get this over with,' Dante commanded and, clasping her hand in his, he led her up and into her own house.

'Wait a minute.' Beth stopped in the large hall and tugged her hand free from his, her palm tingling. She looked frostily up at him. 'I am quite capable of taking care of this myself. In fact I would prefer to.'

'No way. This is my responsibility and I want to know.'

'Are you stupid or what?' Beth demanded in exasperation. 'I am giving you a Get Out of Jail Free card.

You can walk away—forget you ever met me. Most men would leap at the chance.'

'I am not most men, and I can't do that. I remember all too well that we had sex, and if a baby is the result then it is mine as much as yours. Though the thought of being a father, wondering if I will be a good one, *is* worrying.'

Inexplicably Beth's heart squeezed at the hint of vulnerability in the dark gaze he turned on her.

She had not seen Dante look anything but arrogantly sure of himself, and it was a shock to see his big body tense. She realised this was probably even more of a shock for him than for her. Dante Cannavaro was not the type of man who ever made a mistake in his business or personal life and he did not tolerate other people's mistakes. He believed his judgement was infallible, and now he had made a possibly life-changing mistake.... No wonder he looked shaken....

'Take this.' He pressed the pregnancy kit into her hand and glanced around. 'Tell me where the kitchen is and I'll make myself a coffee while you do the test.'

They were standing in the wide hall, which had two doors opening off on either side to the reception rooms. The main focus was a central staircase that divided halfway up and curved into a galleried landing on the first floor.

Beth indicated with one hand to the right of the staircase. 'Down there is the kitchen.'

To her astonishment he wrapped an arm around her shoulders and gave her a hug, dropped a light kiss on her lips. 'Don't worry—it will work out fine either way. I will make sure it does,' he declared, and turned to walk away.

Stunned, Beth looked down at the box in her hand and up again. She wanted to throw it at Dante's back as he strolled off to the kitchen. He was so confident everything would be fine…while she was the opposite— a nervous wreck. But she knew she was only delaying the inevitable and began to ascend the stairs. Her lips were tingling from his kiss, her head was spinning with the enormity of what she was about to do, and her feelings on the result were ambivalent…

Twenty minutes later Beth walked downstairs and entered the kitchen, her face a blank mask. She dropped the test on the table, where Dante sat, and without a word stalked out and down the hall to her sitting room. With a sigh she sank down on the sofa and let her head fall back against the soft cushions.

Binkie padded over to rub against her ankles and Beth's lips quirked at the corners in a brief smile. 'Soon, Binkie, it will no longer be just you and I. There will be a baby as well.' Somehow saying the words out loud finally brought it home to her that she *was* pregnant.

'Amazing. You can tell your damn cat you are pregnant, but I get the test thrown at me.'

Beth glanced up to find Dante bristling with anger, staring down at her. Her own temper rose at the injustice of it all. 'I love my cat, whereas *you* I could not give a damn about. And whichever way you get the news delivered the answer is the same—and it is *your* fault. If you hadn't tracked me down to tell me I might be pregnant I wouldn't have realised for ages, and when I did I definitely would *not* have told you,' she spat, her pent-up emotions finally boiling over. 'It seems to be your goal in life to try to destroy mine. First you are instrumental in sending me to prison, then you try to chase me out of my apartment with your threats and finally you seduce me. A hat-trick is the term in football, I believe. But as I am pregnant it seems you have scored an own goal.'

Beth spoke derisively, but inside she was falling apart. This morning she had got out of bed, happily looking forward to the day ahead. Then Dante had turned her life upside down yet again.

Dante, like most Italian males, was mad about football, and his lips twitched at her last comment. She was sitting down, her arms folded across her middle—which pushed her perfect breasts upwards. Not that they needed any help. His blood heated at the thought.

Damn it, how could one redheaded woman have such an instant effect on his libido? This was serious.

'Look on me as the villain if you must,' he said curtly. 'But it does not alter the fact that you are expecting a baby, and as the father I intend to be fully involved with my child, with or without you…understand?'

Beth looked up at Dante, towering over her, and let her eyes trace the hard bones of his tanned face, the cool, determined eyes, the powerful jaw and tight mouth.

'Yes.' She understood all right. It was what she had feared when he had dropped the bombshell on her a few hours ago. But this time she was ready for him. It was amazing how knowing she was having a baby gave her strength, and she determined to fight him anyway she could. 'That is easy for you to say, but have you really thought this through, Dante?'

Beth deliberately drawled his name, looking up at him through the veil of her long lashes.

'After all, you are an extremely powerful and extremely wealthy man, according to Tony. What will your friends think when they discover the mother of your child is a convicted drug dealer *you* sent to prison? You threatened me with the press. I can do the same.' She saw his dark brows shoot up in surprise. 'Not so nice, is it, when a threat goes against you?' she opined. 'When you demanded I kept out of Tony's life you labelled me as some kind of *femme fatale*. So maybe I decided *you* were a better bet and deliberately allowed you to seduce me in the hope of getting pregnant and getting your money. Can you live with that?'

Dante felt a muscle begin to beat in his temple. It was anger, but it was something else as well. Her spirited attempt to defy him and the sultry look from her green eyes shouldn't have anywhere near the sensual impact it did. The cynic in him *had* had the fleeting thought that Beth might have got pregnant deliberately for money, but he had quickly dismissed the notion as he'd recalled every moment in her bed: the silken caress of her hands against his flesh, the taste and the scent of her. He hadn't been able to get enough of her. And it was making him want to repeat the experience with an urgency that was growing painful.

With that in mind, he lowered his long length on the sofa and slid his arm along the back of the sofa behind her. He noted her flinch. 'An interesting scenario, Beth, but I don't believe you would reveal to the world your criminal past to thwart me, knowing your child would eventually suffer from the knowledge. As for money— it is not something that bothers me. Right now I want to get acquainted with our baby.'

He was right, damn him, and Beth's breath caught

in her throat at *our baby*—and at the gleam she saw in his dark eyes as they moved down her body.

'May I?'

He placed his hand on her still-flat stomach and for a long moment a strange quivering trance held them both as the enormity of what they had created finally sank in.

Dante raised his head, his dark eyes meeting hers, and she was vaguely aware that his other hand was resting on her shoulder. His long fingers stroked her midriff, tenderly edging higher, and suddenly a trance of a different nature shimmered between them.

His arm tightened around her shoulders. His mouth brushed gently across her lips. His hand moved to cup her breast. Beth caught her breath and his mouth covered hers, his tongue stroking along the curve of her lips to seek entry. Her eyes fluttered closed as he kissed her long and deeply, with a seductive tenderness she had never felt before.

Dante raised his head and Beth stared dazedly into his molten eyes as his long fingers circled her neck to trail down her throat, their touch caressing and arousing. Then with a groan his sensuous mouth found hers again, to kiss her with a deepening passion, and his tactile fingers reached the swift rise and fall of her breasts to pluck at one tight nipple. Her lips parted on a low moan as his mouth caught its partner to lick and suckle, and a shaft of sensual pleasure shot through her slender body. Her mind demanded she tell him to stop, but her body was brought vibrantly alive by his touch.

He raised his head and she saw the passionate intent in his dark eyes as she heard his voice. 'You want this, Beth?'

The question and the sound of his deep, husky voice

broke the trance she was in and made Beth realise what she was inviting. 'No!' she cried, and scrambled along the sofa, fighting to catch her breath and still her frantically racing heart. Suddenly she realised the straps of her dress were halfway down her arms, baring her breasts to his avid gaze. How or when it had happened she had no idea....

She could not look at him. She was mortified at how easily she had succumbed to his skilful caress. She pulled the straps of her dress back over her shoulders. The fabric hurt her sensitized breasts, but nowhere near as much as she hurt inside.

Finally she glanced sideways at Dante. He had straightened up, his head resting on the back of the sofa, and she could see the pulse beating in his strong throat, the rise and fall of his muscular chest and the unmistakable bulge in his jeans....

Swallowing hard, she looked away. Knowing she was not the only one suffering was some consolation, and she hoped it hurt. She could not believe she had almost made the same mistake again....

Was she destined to be fatally attracted to this man for the rest of her life? Had his fiancée, Ellen, felt the same? The thought came out of nowhere and made Beth feel worse. Their engagement had been broken the weekend of the barbecue, she knew. But they could be back together by now. They *had* to love each other if they had been arranging the wedding.

A large hand cupped her chin and turned her head, so she was forced to look up at Dante. 'Given your initial response, I don't believe "once was enough" after all,' he drawled, a hint of humour in the dark eyes that held hers. 'I know you, Beth, and I was right. You are a tease, but you also have a natural talent for sex. It is only your stubborn determination to hold a grudge against me that is stopping you. But I can wait.' And he grinned.

It was the grin that got her. She knocked his hand away and leapt off the sofa to stare down at him for a change. 'And you would know because you are such an expert. Tell me, what is Ellen going to say when she discovers you've made me pregnant? Weren't you two supposed to be getting married this month? Or maybe you are not my baby's father? Have you thought of that? I could have had another man since you.' Mentally she kicked herself for not thinking of that sooner.

'No, you haven't. You are as transparent as glass in some respects, and the idea of another man has only just occurred to you—too late to be believed, I'm afraid.' There was no humour in his eyes now, she noted, as he added, 'As for Ellen—she is none of your concern or mine any more. We broke up and the wedding was cancelled, remember?'

'So just like that you dismiss the woman who loved you?' Beth said, dropping the 'other man' plan as pointless. Even if he believed her a DNA test would prove otherwise, and Dante was nothing if not thorough.

'Grow up, Beth. Love had nothing to do with my relationship with Ellen. I decided it was time I got married and Ellen and I are in the same profession, with the same background. She seemed the perfect candidate. We were compatible. I wanted a child, an heir, and she said she wanted the same—until she got emotional and told me I didn't love her enough, threw the engagement ring back at me. I realised she wanted a lot more than I was able to give.'

'How can you be so calculating? I'm not surprised she broke off the engagement!'

'Easily. And I've just realised that now you are pregnant my problem is solved. I have no need to look further. I want this child, and I will pay you whatever you want, whatever it takes, for you to have a healthy baby.'

At his mention of money again Beth's eyes widened in horror as she realised what he really meant. Dante was lounging there, his face enigmatic, as he casually offered to *buy* her baby—which underscored exactly how little he thought of her as a prospective mother.

'I am sure we can come to an acceptable arrangement between us that we can both live with comfortably,' he continued coolly.

'I very much doubt that. And as I can only be eight weeks pregnant it is far too early even for a ruthless devil like you to suggest *buying* my baby,' she said, eyeing him with bitter contempt.

Dante leapt to his feet and his hand shot out. Long, tanned fingers closed round her wrist and he folded her arm around her back to hold her close to his taut body. 'I never suggested buying the baby. Only you and your twisted mind could think such a thing,' he snarled.

For a moment Beth could not move, could not speak. All she could do was feel… The warmth of his breath against her face, the surge of heated emotions battling inside her… Angrily, she was aware that not many minutes ago she had almost succumbed to his lethal sex appeal. If anyone had a twisted mind it was Dante, she thought, recognising the disgust in his tone and finding her voice.

'That is what it sounded like to me—and there is nothing wrong with my mind,' she said bluntly. 'Plain common sense tells me it is far too soon to be discussing arrangements for the baby.'

'Not for me,' he said between his teeth. 'I intend to get this settled now. And you should know that I always get what I want in the end.'

Beth refused to be afraid. 'Yes, I know better than most that with your implications and lies you will stoop to anything to achieve your own ends. If you had taken more care of your own relationship instead of interfering in your brother's life we wouldn't be in this mess,' she told him scathingly.

His face darkened and he held her tighter still to his long body. 'What is done is done—and don't you *ever* think of or refer to our baby as a *mess*.' He threaded his other hand in her hair and tipped her head back, staring down into her defiant face with black searching eyes. 'I know you for what you are, Beth—a beautiful woman with a less-than-salubrious past. Not the sort of woman I would have chosen as the mother of my child, I admit, but you are, and I accept that—and I accept that you have succeeded in living down your mistakes. It is time you accept me as the father, stop flinging insults and start thinking of what is best for our unborn child. I have told you I will provide you with everything—a home where you can live in the lap of luxury and devote all your time to looking after our baby. That is how it is going to be. Understand?'

His head dropped and as though compelled he brought his mouth down on hers, his hand sweeping up her back to splay across her bare shoulder blade with a pressure that flattened her against him.

The long, demanding kiss inflamed Beth's senses, and though she fought to resist her eyes closed involuntarily and she gave in to the persuasive power of his sensuous mouth. When he pulled his head back her arms were wrapped around his waist and her soft lips were parted. Realising what she had done yet again, she dropped her arms, her hands curling into fists at her sides, and stared up at him, trying to read the look in his narrowed gaze. She caught a gleam of desire and some other emotion that she did not recognise.

'Why did you kiss me?' Beth broke the taut silence between them, trying to appear nonchalant while battling the force of feelings his kiss had aroused.

'Because I can't keep my hands off you,' Dante responded—and it was the truth. When he should be comforting Beth, reassuring her, all he could think of was stripping her naked and thrusting into her sleek, hot body as fast and deep as he could.... 'Or maybe to get you to listen,' he added, trying to ignore the throbbing in his groin.

Surprised by his admission that he could not keep his hands off her, and still held against his hard-muscled frame, Beth was intensely aware of Dante in a basic carnal way. The strength of his erection was very evident, she realised, which made her hot and angry with herself almost as much as she was with him.

'I did listen.' She desperately latched on to his last words and added what she hoped were some stinging ones of her own. 'You said you will take care of everything. Does that include marrying me, I wonder?' she asked with a sarcastic tilt of a delicate eyebrow. 'I notice a proposal was not on your list.'

'Yes, of course I am going to marry you.' His hands dropped from her, his dark eyes quizzical. 'I thought I had made that obvious? I told you I would provide ev-

erything—money, a house that we can live comfortably in...'

'No! Never in a million years!' Beth exclaimed, horrified by his response. Her sarcasm had backfired spectacularly.

She moved away, shaking her head, and sat carefully
down on the one armchair in the room, determined to
take control of the situation.

'I only mentioned marriage to make you see sense
and face facts. For a cool, staid lawyer you have been
acting like a man possessed from the moment you arrived here, and I've let you drag me along with you.
But the reality is I am not even nine weeks pregnant,
and anything can happen in the first twelve weeks. I
don't need this conversation now. I need to get used to
the idea of a baby and relax and rest by myself. Get in
touch with me in a few weeks' time, if you must, and
we can discuss the situation then. If that inconveniences
you, then tough. But I am definitely not marrying you.
This is *my* body, *my* baby, and that is how it is going
to be.' And it was Beth's turn to add, 'Understand...?'

Dante ran his hand distractedly though his hair. He
didn't like hearing it, but she could be right. He had
told himself he needed to know she was *not* pregnant so
he could move on. But dashing down here to confront
Beth and drive her to a pharmacy was completely out
of character. It was important to Dante that he stayed
focused on his work and in control of his private life
without compromising the first for the second. His father had taught him that at a young age, and he had
rigidly adhered to that philosophy. He was not going
to change now.

But neither was he going to allow Beth 'weeks' on

her own. Going by her past behavior, and what he knew now, she wasn't wealthy by his standards, but she *had* inherited a healthy amount of money along with this house. She could disappear anytime she liked, and he wasn't taking that chance.

'I understand your reasoning, and that you want some time to accept the fact you are about to become a mother.' He frowned, noting the slight violet shadows beneath the wide eyes she raised to his. The wary expression in the green depths made him grimace. 'I have to be in Rome tomorrow and I want you to come with me. I will ensure you see the best doctor there is, and you can stay at my place in the country. The house is fully staffed and you will be well looked after. You can rest there.'

After which she was going to marry him whether she liked it or not. A civil ceremony could be arranged in two or three weeks....

'No, thank you. I have my own doctor and I prefer my own home.'

Dante noted the determined tilt of her chin and his lips twisted. He wasn't surprised she had refused. In spite of her shady past she was still incredibly naive in some ways. It was obvious the thought of getting pregnant had never crossed her mind until he had mentioned it, and it must have come as a hell of a shock to her when she discovered she was. He had no intention of leaving until he had got her to agree to marry him, but he could wait a while.

'I can see you have a nice house here, but it is rather isolated for a woman alone.'

'I am not alone. I have friends, and I am perfectly

capable of making my own arrangements without any help from you,' Beth said bluntly.

Dante was standing two feet away, his dark eyes holding hers, his deep voice sounding concerned, but she did not trust him. From the first moment she had seen Dante in court she had felt an instant affinity with him and had believed it was hope, but now she was beginning to believe it could be something much more dangerous to her in the long run.

'What arrangements?' Dante demanded, his sensuous lips thinned into an uncompromising hardness and his voice no longer gentle.

Slowly Beth stood up. Dante was not and never could be her friend. He had his own agenda and had actually said that one of his reasons for marrying Ellen had been to get an heir. Beth being pregnant had solved that problem for him.

'Obviously seeing my doctor is first on the agenda. He will book me into the local hospital, which has an excellent reputation.' She stepped towards him. 'Now we have got that settled you can leave. See yourself out.' She paused, waiting for him to move.

Without a word Dante stood aside to let her past. Beth could have her space but it would be a few minutes—certainly not weeks. He was absolutely determined she would marry him, and he knew he did not have time to waste. He was proud of the Cannavaro name and over two hundred years of family history. There was no way a child of his was being born illegitimate.

CHAPTER SEVEN

BETH WALKED PAST DANTE and headed for the kitchen. She was suddenly ravenous. She checked the fridge and withdrew a carton of eggs, two slices of ham, a chunk of cheese and the makings of a salad from the vegetable box. She placed them on the kitchen bench along with some herbs, and then took out the omelette pan and placed it on the hob.

'Can I help?'

She had not heard Dante walk in, and glanced over her shoulder to find him right behind her. 'No. You have done more than enough already,' she said dryly. 'And I thought I told you to leave?'

'I have not eaten since I left London this morning. I suppose I could stop at the local pub for lunch. Bill seems a hospitable guy, and he obviously likes you. He told me where to find you. He'd probably appreciate being the first to know you are pregnant.'

'No. I don't want anyone to know—not until the pregnancy is confirmed by a doctor.' Beth was clinging to straws, she knew. 'Take a seat.' She nodded her head towards the kitchen table. 'I suppose I can feed you before you go. Cheese and ham omelette with salad is all I've got.' She was babbling again, but Dante was too big and too close, and he made her very generously sized kitchen feel like a rabbit hutch.

'Thanks.'

To her relief he moved to pull out a chair and sit down at the table.

Beth placed the salad bowl on the table, along with condiments and cutlery. Then she broke six eggs into a bowl, and in a matter of minutes had heated the oil in the pan and cooked the omelettes. Placing one on each plate, she crossed to the table and put them down, pulling out a chair to sit opposite Dante.

'Enjoy,' she said automatically and, picking up a knife and fork, cut into the fluffy omelette and ate in silence.

'That was delicious,' Dante said, and she looked up to see he had cleaned his plate. 'You really can cook.' A genuine smile indented the lines around his mouth, and there was a gleam of surprise in the dark eyes that met hers.

'Don't sound so surprised! My mother taught me and she was a brilliant cook.' Beth's eyes softened as she remembered. 'Mum made the most gorgeous cakes— probably the reason I was a bit plump as a child.' With food in her stomach and the shock of her situation fading a little, she smiled wryly. 'But after she died the weight began to fall off.'

Dante's breath caught at her gentle smile. 'I am sorry you lost your parents so young, Beth,' he said compassionately. 'I didn't realise your parents had died only a year before your trial. I understand how grief can make people behave irrationally....'

'Oh, please stop. I don't need false sympathy from *you*,' Beth mocked, her shoulders tensing, her green eyes blazing at him. 'And don't insult my intelligence. I was innocent and I was stitched up by Bewick and his friend—and you made sure of it. Tell me, how many more innocent people have you sent to jail? Have you any idea?'

Dante prided himself on his integrity and his honour and was deeply insulted, but he was not about to argue with Beth when she was carrying his child. Instead he stated the facts. 'None. You were found guilty by the jury, not me. As a lawyer, I did what I was hired to do—make the case to the best of my ability on the evidence presented by the police and witnesses, not just you. There was nothing personal about it and any other decent lawyer would have got the same result on the evidence. It was also my last criminal case. International commercial litigation is my specialty.'

Beth's eyes widened incredulously on his darkly brooding face. 'I was your last criminal case? That *really* makes me feel a whole lot better,' she said in a voice dripping with sarcasm. 'You said it without a trace of irony and you sound so plausible—but then that *is* your forte.'

'You will think what you want.' For an instant an expression she did not recognise flashed in the depths of his dark eyes and was gone. 'In my experience women usually do.'

Beth shoved back her chair and stood up. 'You are such a chauvinist,' she said, and picked the plates up from the table.

'Well, I don't wash dishes,' he quipped.

She almost smiled as she carried them to the sink, put in the plug and turned on the tap. Idly, she swirled the water around with her hand, then turned off the tap and added some liquid soap, mulling over in her head what Dante had told her.

Maybe he had a point when he said it was nothing personal. He probably spent most of his life in a court-room and must have had hundreds if not thousands of cases. He could not possibly remember all the people involved.

Beth grimaced. He had not remembered her at the barbecue and probably never would have done if not for Tony's joke about marrying her, which had made Dante suspect she was after his brother and his money. She, on the other hand, had recognised Dante the first time she'd seen him again in the street as the man who had haunted her dreams for years. So what did that say about *her*?

Strangely, it put things into perspective for Beth. The day she had left prison Helen had told her not to look back, never to let bitterness affect her new life… But at her trial Beth had fixated on Dante and blamed him personally for the result. She had hated him for years. Now she realised that, given the evidence against her, she would have got the same result with another lawyer. Not that it made any difference. Dante was still the su-premely confident, arrogant man he had always been.

She rinsed off the plates and the pan and stood them on the drainer, then turned around at the sound of his voice. He had his cell phone to his ear and was talking in rapid-fire Italian, his other hand gesturing wildly. He looked and sounded so animated and so very foreign to her, and she felt an odd twinge in her heart.

He lifted his head, a smile still curving his lips. 'Work,' he said, and slipped the phone in his jeans pocket.

Beth caught her breath. She was tempted to smile back, and that frightened her. He was a handsome, charismatic man when it suited him, but she had seen the dark side of him—the clever, domineering and unbelievable bossy character—and she needed to get rid of him....

'You know, Dante, I have hated you for years and now I realise it was a wasted emotion,' she said, schooling her features into a blank mask. 'You will never change and you are always right—which does not bode very well for the future of my baby. An autocratic father is the last thing a child needs. And I really think you should go now.'

'I agree. But I want you to come with me. I don't like the idea of leaving you on your own here.'

'I won't be on my own. I told you Janet and Annie are coming to stay and we are going out for the rest of the day.' She flashed him a smile that did not reach her eyes. 'Have a safe journey.'

Beth turned back to the sink and pulled out the plug, watched the water drain away.

She heard the scrape of a chair on the floor. Good, he was going.... Hopefully by the time she saw Dante again—if she saw him again—she would have a plan to deal with him. Maybe a monthly visit...something like that. Firmly settled in her new life, with people around her she trusted, the thought of having a baby was not so scary after all. In fact she was thrilled, and loved the baby already. Working from her own home was the perfect solution for a single mother. No nursery, no childcare and a great environment to bring up her child.

Beth picked up a teatowel and dried her hands and turned around to make sure Dante had left—only to see him standing in front of the table, his steely gaze focused on her.

'I thought you'd gone.' Her eyes clashed with his and a sliver of fear trickled down her spine. He still exuded an aura of firmly controlled masculine power, and yet she sensed something had shifted. She felt the heightened tension in the air, saw the hard resolution in his dark eyes, and resisted the urge to moisturise her suddenly dry lips.

'I don't take orders, but when I give them I expect them to be obeyed—something you will have to learn when we are married.'

'Married?' she parroted dumbly.

'Yes, married.'

Beth was shocked rigid for a moment. To want to marry her after all that had been said between them— he must be crazy....

Stony-faced, she squared her shoulders and bravely held his gaze. 'Let me make this very clear. I am not marrying you. I'd have to be out of my mind to marry a man who thinks I am a criminal or a *femme fatale* who preys on young men. And my opinion of you is as bad—if not worse. I don't *like* who and what you are, let alone love you.'

'I am not that keen on you as a wife,' he said dryly. 'But there is a baby to consider. As long as we are civil to each other and concentrate all our energy on giving the child the nurturing and love it deserves I don't see a problem. We are sexually compatible, and in my experience lust is preferable to love—if love even exists, which I doubt.'

Beth felt the colour rise in her cheeks as images of her tussle on the sofa with him filled her mind—and the full-blown sex that had got her into this position in the first place....

'That is the most cold-blooded argument for getting married I have ever heard, and typical of you,' she declared scathingly.

'No, it is eminently sensible. I want my child born legitimately and brought up in Italy, as I was, on the family estate. But I travel abroad a lot, and spend quite a bit of my time in London, so I don't mind if you keep this house and stay here when I'm in the city. So long as you devote all your time to our child.'

His arrogant attitude infuriated Beth. 'No. Marrying you is out of the question. It is never going to happen.'

'As I see it there are only two options. We get married or I take you to court for sole custody of the child— which will be a long, drawn-out process that could go on for years, and you know I will win eventually. You choose.'

Beth felt as if all the air had left her body and she stared at him in horror. He meant it. She recognised the cold, implacable determination in his voice.

'That is no choice at all!' she exclaimed and, taking a steadying breath, she tilted up her chin, just as determined as Dante. 'My mother—whoever she was—abandoned me as a baby in a hospital emergency department. Much as I loved my adoptive parents, I would never give up custody of my child. But I certainly would not fight you in court after the last time. I'm not that stupid. I know what a devious devil you can be and I have little faith in your sort of justice. As for marrying you? Spending the rest of my life with *you* does not bear thinking about.'

Dante had not realised she was adopted. The investigator had not gone that far back. But in her last comment his fertile mind saw a way to get what he wanted...

'Then don't think about the rest of your life. Nothing lasts for ever,' he stated with a cynical arch of a black brow. 'And though I am not in favour of divorce, under the circumstances I am prepared to make allowances. If by the time the child is three—old enough to really know its parents—you find married life intolerable, I will give you an amicable divorce with shared custody of the child. In fact I will draw up a prenuptial agreement stating as much.'

Beth's eyes widened a fraction. Her first thought had been to dismiss marriage out of hand, but now Dante had surprised and shocked her. Had he said it deliberately? she wondered, and studied him for a moment. His expression was watchful but not malicious, she decided. A wry smile played around her lips. He was so insensitive, so self-centred, that he did not recognise the irony in offering her a divorce after three years. Her prison sentence had been three years....

'A marriage with a get-out clause you mean?' she said, and amazingly she found herself considering it. She had done one prison sentence because of him, and got out after eighteen months. Who was to say she could not get out of the marriage sentence sooner? While loving her child she could be the wife from hell. Making Dante's life a misery would be sweet revenge for all he had put her through....

He continued to look at her with that unwavering dark gaze. 'Yes, exactly as I stated.'

Beth wanted the best for her child, and though she hated to admit it Dante's offer was probably the best she was going to get. She would not have to stay in Italy all the time, as he had said. He spent quite a lot of time travelling all over the place with his work. Dante might be the biological father of her baby, but she couldn't see him being a hands-on father. In fact she might not see much of him at all, she realised. She glanced around the kitchen, her brain ticking over.

'Do I have any choice?' she questioned cynically.

'You know the alternative. Is that what you want?'

'No, definitely not,' Beth said. She could see no other way out....

Dante caught her shoulders and stared grimly down at her.

'Then make up your mind. What is it to be? Yes or no?'

'Then yes, I suppose,' she said fatalistically. 'But I want an iron-clad pre—'

A voice cut her off.

'Hey, Beth—that is some car outside. Do you know whose it is?' Janet asked as she walked into the kitchen with Annie. She stopped dead, her gaze settling on Dante, still holding Beth.

'No,' Beth said quickly. 'Yes, I mean. This is...'

She stopped as Dante dropped a swift kiss on her lips, let go of her and moved to Janet.

'Allow me to introduce myself. I'm Dante, a very close friend of Beth's, hoping soon to be much more. You must be Janet,' Dante said smoothly, and Beth stared open-mouthed with shock as he smiled and took her friend's hand. 'Beth has told me so much about you. It is a pleasure to finally meet you and your adorable little girl, Annie.'

'Oh...oh, hello,' Janet stuttered. Overawed by his formidable presence she turned huge blue eyes on Beth.

'You dark horse, Beth. I didn't know you had a boy-friend.'

'We met years ago and renewed our relationship ear-lier this year, but Beth likes to keep me hidden,' Dante declared outrageously. 'While I want her to come to Italy for a holiday to show her my world and persuade her to marry me.'

Beth could not believe the glib devil, and watched as he bestowed a megawatt smile on Janet the like of which she had never seen before.

'Ah, a Latin lover—I should have guessed.' Janet turned to her, and much to Beth's chagrin she blushed. 'Beth, I can't believe you never once mentioned this gor-geous man. I can't say I blame you. If he was mine I'd keep him to myself as well.' She grinned and glanced admiringly back up at Dante.

Beth silently groaned. Janet was a great friend, but hopelessly outspoken. 'You don't understand…' she began.

'What's to understand? A holiday in Italy sounds great to me—and the man hopes to marry you! Accept quickly, before he changes his mind.'

'I can't just take off to Italy. I can't leave Binkie, and the builders are going to start on the conversion soon.'

'Don't worry. I'll take care of Binkie. And as for the conversion—you can have at least two weeks holiday before it starts.'

Somehow, ten minutes later, Beth found herself standing by the Bentley with Dante, her future more or less decided.

He kissed her—for Janet's benefit, she guessed—then told her he would call her the next day to confirm arrangements. He already had her house phone number, and he gave her his card with a list of numbers where she could contact him. She supposed she should be grateful he did not whisk her away there and then. At least she had a couple of days to think of an alternative.

By the time Beth went to bed that night she was exhausted, but her head was filled with the events of the day and she could not sleep. Janet had asked her umpteen questions but Beth hadn't had the heart to tell her that she was pregnant. In fact she was having a hard time accepting it herself. As for Dante saying he was hoping to persuade her to marry him—she didn't know why he bothered prevaricating.... He had left her no choice *but* to marry him.

Beth called Clive the next day and told him she was going on holiday to Italy for two weeks. She hadn't the nerve to tell him the truth, and was still hoping it would all miraculously go away. She told him she would ring him when she got back, but he said he was going away himself on a three-month lecture tour around the universities in Australia, and somehow Beth felt more alone than ever.

It was two o'clock on Friday afternoon when Beth stepped off the plane in Rome. She was met by a uniformed gentleman who whisked her through Customs, telling her that her baggage would be taken care of, and ushered her into a VIP lounge, informing her that Signor Cannavaro was to meet her there.

Beth had never flown first-class before—in fact she had only ever flown four times. Nervously she smoothed the oatmeal cashmere dress she wore down over her hips and looked around. There were a few business types, but no sign of Dante. With a bit of luck he might have changed his mind and she could go back to England straight away, instead of in two weeks' time as Dante had agreed.

Dante's meeting had run on for longer than he'd expected, and the traffic to the airport was horrendous. He stopped at the open door of the lounge at the sight of Beth, walking down the room. She was wearing a long-sleeved sweater dress that followed every seductive line of her body to end above her knees, and high-heeled shoes accentuated her fabulous legs. She looked sensational, and a vivid image of those legs wrapped around his waist, his body buried to the hilt in hers, filled his mind.

He took a deep, steadying breath to control his raging libido and moved forward, noticing that every other man in the place was watching her. For a moment he saw red....

Beth was beginning to wonder if Dante really had changed his mind. There was still no sign of him and she looked again at her wristwatch.

'Beth, *cara*.'

She heard his voice and turned to see him walking towards her. Butterflies took up a war dance in her stomach and her breath caught in her throat. He was wearing a charcoal suit, white shirt and striped tie, and for such a big, powerfully built man he moved with the lithe ease of an athlete. He looked fabulous—but he also looked furious, she realised.

His hands caught her shoulders and a firm male mouth descended on her parted lips. She lifted a hand to press against the hard wall of his chest, but for some reason her fingers spread out over the soft silk of his shirt.

It was Dante who ended the kiss. 'I'm sorry I'm late, but did you *have* to parade up and down the lounge?'

'Parade?' Beth queried, her green gaze flicking up over the hard planes of his handsome face, his smooth tanned skin and square jaw. She saw masculine strength and, surprisingly, bewilderment in his extraordinary dark eyes.

Dante shook his head. 'I can't believe I said that. You are an impossible woman, Beth.' Taking her arm, he added, 'Come on—let's get out of here.' And he marched her out of the airport so fast she almost had to run to keep up with him.

Five minutes later a chauffeur held open the passenger door of a sleek black limousine, and Dante told her to get in quickly.

Beth sat in the back, as far away from Dante as she could get. It was warmer in Italy than she had expected, and the cashmere dress had not been a good choice, so she was grateful for the air conditioning. She glanced across at him and the resentment she had bottled up since the last time she saw him got the better of her. 'You gave me only days to prepare to come here for a holiday I don't want, and now you race me out of the airport like a marathon man. What's the rush?'

'You have a doctor's appointment and we are going to be late.'

'What doctor's appointment?' Beth demanded, glaring at him.

'The one I have made for you. Don't worry—he is the top man in Rome.'

'Wait a minute. I thought you said I was staying at

your home in the country? In any case I can't step off a plane and go straight to a doctor.'

A frown lined his broad brow. 'Why not? The sooner you see a doctor the better. I want confirmation that the baby is fine before I take you to the countryside.'

'Yes, I see your point,' Beth said—and she did. He wanted to make absolutely certain she was pregnant before he married her. Well, that was fine by her. She didn't want to marry him any more than he wanted to marry her. They were only doing it for the baby.

It was obviously a private clinic, and Dr Pascal was a lovely man who spoke English, much to Beth's relief. He asked them both a few questions, and the only awkward moment came when he asked Beth if she knew of any hereditary illnesses in her family. For a moment she was lost for words.

'My fiancée was adopted at birth,' Dante answered for her, and reached for her hand, squeezing it reassuringly. 'So she can't answer that.'

'Never mind. I have enough information.' He called a nurse in and asked her to take Beth to the examination room, and told Dante to wait in his office.

When Beth finally followed the doctor back into the office Dante leapt to his feet. 'Is everything all right, Doctor?' he demanded, not even glancing at her.

For some reason—maybe because it had finally sunk in that the baby was real—she felt hurt that he had not spoken to *her*.

The doctor smiled. 'Everything is perfect, Signor Cannavaro—the baby is fine. You are a lucky man.' He turned admiring eyes on Beth and then back to Dante. 'Your fiancée is an extremely fit and healthy young woman about nine weeks pregnant. I have made an appointment for a scan in two weeks' time.'

Dante showed no emotion as he thanked the doctor in Italian. They spoke for a few moments longer and then they left.

Beth slid back into the limousine and stared out of the window as it manoeuvred through the Rome traffic, oblivious to the city's great landmarks, lost in her own thoughts. In the days since Dante had burst back into her life and she'd discovered she was pregnant she had not been absolutely certain that it was real, but now there was no doubt. A child deserved to be born with love, not this way, she thought sadly.

'So there is no going back,' Dante stated. 'If you give me your passport I can complete the arrangements for a civil marriage in Rome in two weeks. Under the circumstances we will not inform friends or family until after the fact.'

Beth's spine straightened, her eyes widening in shock. There was not a hint of softness or real emotion in Dante's hard gaze. 'Surely we do not need to rush into marriage? It makes more sense to wait until the child is born.'

'Maybe with any other woman, but I am not taking a chance with you. You are a flight risk. You have already changed your identity once, you have no family, no employer, no real ties of any kind, and you are not exactly penniless. You could disappear at any time, and I can't spare the time to track you down again.'

'You—you...'

Beth spluttered furiously. 'What is to stop me taking off *after* we are married? Or do you intend to keep me a prisoner for the next three years?'

'Nothing so dramatic,' Dante drawled in a mocking undertone. 'Once we are married I would not have to waste *my* time looking for you. You'd be a missing wife and the forces of law would do it for me.'

Beth sucked in air. She wanted to kill him, but she couldn't even trust herself to speak.

'We will marry in two weeks, as I said, and I will fly back with you to London on Sunday and introduce you to my mother as my wife. Then we will return to your cottage in time for the builders' arrival on Monday...agreed?'

'Agreed,' Beth murmured, her face expressionless. She opened her bag, withdrew her passport and handed it to Dante. Her fingers brushed his and she flinched. For the first time since Helen had died Beth felt like crying. Hormones, she told herself, and took a deep breath.

'Are you all right?' Dante queried, dark brown eyes narrowing on her face. 'You look tired.'

'Yes. You heard the doctor—I'm fine. But it is good of you to be concerned.' If he noticed the sarcasm in her voice she didn't care. All she cared for was the baby.

The rest of the journey was conducted in almost complete silence. Beth was simmering with resentment at the position Dante had put her in, which was not helped by the self-satisfied look on his handsome face....

'Beth, wake up—we have arrived.'

Her eyes fluttered open and she realised she was held in the protective curve of Dante's arm, her head on his chest. Then she shot up and smoothed the skirt of her dress over her thighs, mortified that she had fallen asleep on him, and—worse—that she had enjoyed the comforting feeling.

CHAPTER EIGHT

BETH STEPPED OUT of the car and glanced around. It was dark, but she had a brief glimpse of the façade of the house, and large double doors standing open, sending a broad beam of light into the night as Dante took her arm and led her inside.

Dante introduced her to Sophie, his housekeeper, and her husband, Carlo, and three more staff whose names she didn't register as he walked her across the marble floor to a grand staircase.

'I'll show you to your room.' He glanced at his wrist-watch. 'You have forty-five minutes to settle in. Sophie insists on serving dinner no later than nine, and as she has worked here since before I was born I don't dare argue with her.'

'That's good of you,' Beth said with a surprised smile, and her smile broadened when Dante ushered her into her room. It was unmistakably feminine, all white and pastel pink, with painted antique furniture, and definitely not the master bedroom—which was a huge relief to her.

'Thank you. This is a lovely room.'

'Don't thank me, thank Sophie. It was her choice.

I told her a female friend was staying for a couple of weeks and obviously she is trying to impress you.'

'I will,' Beth murmured as he left.

Carlo arrived with her luggage and a maid, who showed her the dressing room and bathroom.

Fifteen minutes later, feeling refreshed and slightly more relaxed, Beth stepped out of the shower and wrapped a soft white towel around her before walking into the dressing room. The staff were gone and her luggage was unpacked, and she quickly found the drawer that contained her lingerie, withdrawing matching white lace briefs and bra and slipping them on.

Sitting at the dressing table, she brushed her hair and applied moisturiser to her face. With a flick of mascara to her long lashes and a touch of tinted gloss to her lips she was ready.

After exactly forty-five minutes Beth descended the staircase to the hall, wearing a knee-length wraparound green jersey silk dress that tied in a bow at the side, and black kitten-heeled shoes.

Reaching the bottom of the stairs, she looked around the huge reception hall. She tried the first of two doors on the left and was relieved to see it was the dining room. She walked in and paused.

Standing by a marble fireplace, a glass in his hand, was Dante.

'Drinking already!' she blurted, insanely disturbed by the sight of Dante in a black lounge suit. His stunning physical presence was almost overwhelming, and suddenly she was no longer relaxed but tense.

'I could say you are enough to drive any man to drink in that dress,' he responded, his dark eyes roaming appreciatively over her as he crossed to where she stood and took her arm. 'You look beautiful.'

'Thank you,' she murmured. The warmth of his strong hand on her arm was sending her pulse haywire. She was just about holding herself together, but if he didn't let go of her soon she was liable to melt in a puddle at his feet—or strangle him. Dante infuriated her and fascinated her in equal measure. He was like a force of nature—magnificent but sometimes deadly....

Minutes later, with Dante seated at the top of a long dining table and Beth to his right, Sophie appeared with the first course. Carlo followed with the wine and offered to fill her glass.

Beth said water would be fine for her.

Dante's dark brows rose, but as realisation hit him an approving smile curved his firm lips. 'Which would you prefer, Beth? Sparkling or still?'

'Still water, please.' Shaking out her napkin, she put it on her lap.

Sophie served the meal—a plate of delicious antipasta, followed by a tasty mushroom risotto and then perfectly seasoned sea bass.

Dante drank wine and kept her glass topped up with water, and made easy, informative conversation. Beth learned his was a working estate, which included a vineyard, and he regaled her with stories of his childhood— how as a six-year-old he had tried to tread grapes in a bucket to make his own wine, much to his father's amusement, and other episodes that despite herself made her chuckle.

She mentioned the painting hanging above the fireplace and he told her it was of his father, who had died at the age of fifty-two in a car accident. The paintings in the hall and on the stairway were of his ancestors. Somehow the family portraits brought home to Beth just what she had let herself in for over the next three years....

Beth's appetite had disappeared by dessert—mainly because she was beginning to warm to this relaxed, witty Dante in his home environment and could not relax herself. She found her eyes straying to his mouth, found herself swallowing hard as he unselfconsciously licked his lips.

When he suggested they have coffee in the main salon she pushed back her seat and stood up. 'If you don't mind I'll give the coffee a miss.' She deliberately patted her stomach. 'I'm tired after all the travelling, the doctor and everything. I'd like to go to bed.'

His dark eyes narrowed on her. 'Okay, I'll see you to your room.'

Ascending the stairs with Dante's oddly protective hand on her back, she asked herself how the cool, successful Beth of three months ago could have been dumb enough to get herself in this position. She turned at the door to her room and glanced at Dante, to say goodnight. But the hand at her back slid around her waist, and with his free hand he opened the bedroom door and backed her inside.

'Goodnight, Dante,' she said firmly, and put her hands on his chest to ward him off.

He caught her hands on his shirtfront in one of his much larger ones. 'Surely our relationship warrants a goodnight kiss—?'

'That's not necessary,' she cut in. His dark eyes met hers and she saw the gleam of desire in their black depths. She could not move.

'It is necessary for me,' he said huskily before his mouth captured hers.

It all happened so fast. One minute she was outside her room, saying goodnight, and the next she was inside, held against Dante's long body, her hands flailing ineffectually at him. But with humiliating speed her resistance faded under the seductive persuasion of his lips. Her hands were no longer hitting him but clasping his broad shoulders, and a soft moan escaped her as his mouth drew her deeper into the kiss.

Dante raised his head, his glittering gaze skimming over her. His eyes lingered on the curve of her breasts revealed by the wrap-over neckline of her dress, and he slipped light fingers beneath the white lace bra to stroke and shape a burgeoning peak. 'I like your lingerie, Beth, but I prefer you naked,' he said throatily, and took her lush mouth with his again.

She linked her hands behind his neck as his tongue twined with hers, stoking the heat of arousal simmering inside her. Beth was aware only of Dante, of the heady taste of him, the pleasure of his touch driving every conscious thought from her mind.

So it was all the more shocking when suddenly his hands gripped her waist and he physically lifted her to hold her at arm's length.

Limbs weak, she swayed towards him—but his grip tightened and her eyes widened, finally focusing on his harshly handsome face. She saw leashed passion in the dark eyes, but she also saw a determination in the hard line of his mouth that told her the ardent lover was gone and in his place was the autocratic Dante.

'I want you, Beth, and I could have you now. Your body tells me that every time I touch you…. If it is any consolation it is exactly the same for me. The physical chemistry between us is dynamite,' he said bluntly. 'But we need to get a few things straight.'

Battling to control her wayward senses, Beth was mortified—and suddenly becoming aware the bodice of her dress was gaping wider to reveal her bra simply made it worse. Though knowing this fire in the blood, this instant attraction, was the same for him was some consolation. Speechless, she stared at him.

'To make this marriage work we need some ground rules. The first one being obvious. We will have a normal relationship; I am not cut out to be celibate and neither are you.'

Beth tried to adjust the top of her dress.

'No, not tonight,' he said with a hint of self-mockery. 'I can wait until we are married. The doctor told me you are a healthy woman, and that sex won't harm you or the baby.'

'You actually asked the doctor?' Beth finally found her voice.

'Of course. I intend to take good care of you and the child. Which brings me to my second point.' Surprisingly, he let go of her waist and adjusted her dress by tightening the bow at her waist. 'You are far too distracting,' he said with a wry twist of his lips. 'We have to put on a united front in front of friends and family, with all that entails. No flinching away from me would be a good start—especially in public, as I expect you to play the part of my wife to the full. I have also arranged a personal account for you at my bank.'

'That is not necessary.'

'Yes, it is, Beth. No argument. Tomorrow we are going to Milan to purchase a ring and a suitable wardrobe for you. I attend quite a few social functions, and once we are married naturally you will accompany me. I have to return to Rome tomorrow, but I will try to get back next weekend. If not I will be back to collect you the following Friday for your hospital appointment. The civil ceremony will be on Saturday. In the meantime you can rest and relax as you originally suggested. Is everything clear?'

'Yes.' Beth agreed. She was slowly becoming resigned to the fact that her life was going to be inextricably linked to Dante's for years to come. 'Now may I go to bed? I really am tired.'

'Of course. Anything else can wait until tomorrow.' Dante's lips brushed hers. 'Sleep well.' And with a sardonic arch of a black brow he added, 'If you can,' and left.

Beth stood where he had left her and to her shame realised Dante was right. She was too weak to resist her sexy soon-to-be husband. Maybe she shouldn't even try, a little devil on her shoulder whispered. One of her mother's favourite sayings had been, 'You've made your bed and you have to lie in it.' Well, Dante had certainly made hers by getting her pregnant, so why not enjoy the experience while it lasted? How difficult could it be to play the part of Signora Cannavaro as he'd suggested—or more precisely ordered?

Her parents had brought her up well. As an accountant she had wined and dined wealthy clients, mixed with the best and the worst. Sophisticated society didn't faze her at all. And with Dante's track record where women were concerned she had no illusions. He would probably tire of her within months, if not weeks....

But she would still have her child to love and care

for, and that was all that mattered to her. She doubted she would look at another man even when the three years were up.

The sunlight streaming through the window made Beth blink sleepily, and the strong smell of fresh coffee made her eyes fly open and her face pale. She sat up to see Sophie by the bed, a tray in her hands.

'Just leave it on the bedside table, Sophie,' she said weakly. 'I need the bathroom and a shower first.'

'Ah, I understand,' Sophie said, a broad smile lighting her plump face. 'What would you like for breakfast?' she asked.

'Tea and toast will be fine,' Beth said.

She waited till Sophie had left and then slid out of bed, picked up the coffee and headed for the bathroom to tip it down the toilet. Fifteen minutes later, showered and dried, she opened a wardrobe and eyed the contents. What did one wear to shop in Milan, Italy's capital of fashion? she wondered. Her choice of clothes was limited. She had packed a few casual clothes and not much else except for the dress she had worn last night, plus another dress, and one smart suit. After perspiring in the cashmere yesterday, and with the blazing sun this morning in mind, she opted for the linen dress.

Dante was waiting impatiently at the foot of the stairs when Beth came down. He took one look and knew he was in big trouble. She was beautiful and elegant and she took his breath away. He recognised the pale grey dress she wore immediately, and it had the same effect on him now as it had the first time he had seen her wearing it in that London street. But now it was worse. Now he knew what he was missing....

Her glorious red hair fell in natural waves to brush her shoulders. Her make-up was restrained—a touch of eyeshadow, long thick lashes accentuated by mascara, lips glistening with a rose gloss—and her flawless skin positively glowed.

Why the hell hadn't he taken her to bed last night when he'd had the chance? Instead he had set out the rules for their marriage and said no sex until after the wedding. He must have been out of his mind.

Reaching up, he took her arm before she got to the last step.

'Good, you are ready. But what did you do to Sophie? She is dancing around the kitchen with a broad grin on her face, making tea and toast.'

'Good morning to you, too,' Beth said dryly. 'And I didn't do anything to Sophie. She asked me what I wanted for breakfast and I told her. So if you don't mind I'd like to go and eat it before we leave.'

Dante saw Carlo approaching and pressed a swift kiss on her open mouth. 'Fine, *cara*, but make it quick. I'll go and check the helicopter.'

Of *course* Dante would pilot his own helicopter. He always had to be in control, she thought as he strapped her into the seat beside him.

'I though cars were your secret addiction, not helicopters?'

He shot her a slanting smile. 'They are. But anything with an engine floats my boat. Actually, I have a speedboat and a yacht down at my villa in Portofino.'

Beth grinned and shook her head. 'Why doesn't that surprise me?'

The helicopter landed on the top of a tall building, and Beth looked around at the sprawling city below with a growing sense of panic.

Dante urged her into the building. Beth tensed when she saw the elevator. The next minute she was inside, with him standing next to her like a jailer as he pressed the button for the ground floor and the metal doors slid shut. The elevator began to descend, and so did Beth's stomach. She clenched her teeth, every muscle in her body locking in panic, and stared straight ahead.

Dante glanced down at Beth and saw the frozen expression on her face, the tension in her body. 'Are you all right?' he asked, curving an arm around her rigid shoulders.

'Fine. I'm just a bit claustrophobic in elevators—have been ever since I got out of prison. I think it's a light thing. I have no problem with glass ones on the outside of buildings.'

'Why didn't you say so? Most women I know would be shouting it from the treetops, but you barely tell me anything.' It was true, Dante thought, frustrated by her reticence, not only today but since the moment he had met her again.

'What would be the point? You rarely believe anything I say.'

Her eyes were fixed on the control panel and Beth didn't see Dante wince. When the light flashed for the ground floor she was out of his protective arm and through the doors before they were fully open, and she didn't stop until she was on the street.

She took a few deep, steadying breaths. At least she

had not been sick this time, she thought with some relief as Dante once again looped an arm around her waist.

'How are you feeling?' he asked, and tilted her chin up with the tip of his fingers, his dark eyes studying her face.

'Fine. I told you—it's not a problem,' she said, shaking her head to dislodge his fingers from her chin. 'Now, let's go shopping. That's why we're here, isn't it? I need the distraction of some retail therapy.'

'Okay. First the jewellers and the ring,' Dante said as they started walking. 'As it will be a civil ceremony a wedding gown is not necessary, but if you want one...'

'No way,' Beth cut in, shooting him a sidelong glance. 'Sackcloth would do me, but I'll settle for anything you like,' she said dryly.

If only that were true, Dante thought, and a fantasy of Beth naked and bound to his bed flitted through his mind.

Five minutes later they were seated in an exclusive jewellers with an assortment of platinum wedding rings on display in front of them. 'Choose which one you like,' Dante commanded.

'No, you choose,' Beth shot back. 'After all, this is your idea.'

And in two minutes Dante had done just that. To her amazement he'd picked a pair of matching wedding rings and the jeweller had sized them. Dante paid, left his Rome address for them to be delivered to and they left.

'I don't know who was more surprised, the jeweller or me, when you picked those rings,' Beth said as Dante took her hand and they continued walking. 'I didn't see you as the sort of man to wear a wedding ring.'

'Somehow I don't think you see me at all,' Dante said enigmatically, and ushered her into a designer boutique.

While Beth stared around in awe at the elegant interior Dante had a long conversation with two very attentive female assistants.

'Beth?' He came back to where she stood, like patience on a monument. 'These two ladies will take care of you, and you can show me the results.' He lowered his lean, long-limbed body down on a plush sofa and smiled up at her. 'Go on, Beth—we don't have all day.'

'Yes, oh, master,' she mocked. She saw another assistant appear and offer Dante coffee. By the way she fussed over him a lot more was on offer, Beth thought snidely, and turned away. She wondered how many other women he had brought here. He seemed to be well known.

What followed was a revelation to Beth. She paraded before Dante in casual outfits and then suits, day dresses and finally evening dresses. All the time Dante lounged on the sofa, with a smile on his handsome face and a wicked gleam in his dark eyes, making personal comments on the fit and style, thoroughly enjoying himself at her expense. Beth was getting more incensed by the minute.

Finally, wearing a slim-fitting silver evening dress the assistant had virtually poured her into, which clung to her hips and bottom like a second skin, she'd had enough.

'Now, *that* I like. We'll take it,' Dante said, sitting up straighter as she walked towards him.

She slowly turned around and heard his intake of breath at the rear view. Glancing back at him over her shoulder, she saw the stunned look on his face, and a provocative smile curved her lips.

'Are you sure?' she said, and, turning, she sashayed over to him and sat down on his lap. She curled an arm around his broad shoulders and lifted a finger to trace the outline of his firm lips. 'Do you really think this is me?' she asked throatily.

Dante was speechless. Beth approaching him with a smile and touching him was a first. Forgetting where he was, he wrapped his arms around her as she nuzzled his ear, the soft warmth of her breath making him hot.

'Enough is enough,' she hissed vehemently. 'Remember the reason I am here. This dress is a waste of money—I will never get it on in a couple of weeks.'

He turned her head and covered her mouth with his in a fierce kiss.

The kiss caught Beth by surprise. All she could feel was the heat of desire, the pressure of his hand on her bare back and the hardening of his body against her buttocks. When he broke the kiss she was breathless.

'You're right, of course, Beth,' Dante said and, grasping her by the waist, took her with him as he stood up, lowering her down his long body. 'And I was also right. You are a natural-born tease.'

Beth's provocative action was a salutary reminder to him of what she was really like. He had been in danger of forgetting in the shock of her pregnancy. 'Go and get dressed. I'll settle things here. Shopping is over. We are leaving.'

He let her go and walked across to the desk to settle the bill. After a few words with the assistant, he made a phone call to his driver. A few minutes later Beth reappeared. There was no denying she was incredibly lovely, with a perfect figure, he thought clinically, but so were plenty of other women who were *not* ex-cons. He was only marrying her because she was pregnant.

He took her arm and led her outside—and stopped.

Glancing up, Beth tracked where he was looking—at his watch—and when he lifted his eyes to hers they were hard.

'It is only twelve-thirty. We could be home in an hour,' he opined, 'or if you prefer we can lunch here. I do have to be in Rome by this evening, so we will have to be quick.'

'Your home is fine by me,' Beth said, because deep inside she knew it was never going to be *her* home.

'Good. I have had the helicopter moved to a ground-level helipad and a car is picking us up in a minute.'

In other words he had already arranged to leave, making his offer of lunch about as genuine as their marriage was going to be.

It was the longest conversation they were to have on the journey back. The car ride was short, the helicopter was standing in a field, and once on board no conversation was necessary anyway.

It did not get much better when they got back to the house.

Belatedly Beth remembered to thank him for the clothes. Dante simply shrugged and led her into his study, where he presented her with a prenuptial agreement.

'Sit here and read it. I have had it translated from Italian to English. Make a note of anything you want to query. I'll go and tell Sophie to prepare your lunch.'

Beth sat at the desk and started to read. The document was only four pages and quite succinct. Yes, it was there in black-and-white. After three years she could have a divorce and joint custody of their child, and the amount of money he was prepared to give her was enormous. Her first thought was to refuse the money, but common sense prevailed. She might not want his money, but she could think of a lot of people who needed it. She could give it to charity. Dante could certainly afford it.

When Dante came back she told him it was fine, and he took the document and left.

Beth replaced the phone on the bedside table and sighed.

It was odd that she had no trouble talking to Dante on the phone. Since their trip to Milan and his swift return to Rome he had called her most mornings. At first the conversations had been brief, with him just asking how she was, but gradually they had lengthened. He had not come back last weekend, citing pressure of work— much to Sophie's disgust and Beth's relief.

Sophie had shown her around the house and gardens, Carlo the rest of the estate, and Beth had done a lot of exploring on her own. Dante had asked her what she thought of the place, and she'd told him the house and grounds were beautiful. They had discussed all sorts of things, and Beth had found herself enjoying his calls. But now Dante was coming back and she was a bundle of nerves.

CHAPTER NINE

GLANCING AROUND THE feminine bedroom Beth had grown accustomed to, she wondered if she would ever sleep there again. Dismissing the disturbing thought, she slid off the bed and quickly showered and dressed in one of her new purchases—a midnight-blue trouser suit teamed with a heavy white silk blouse. Her own clothes were already in a suitcase, along with a couple of new additions courtesy of Dante. After adding her toiletries she was ready.

A leisurely breakfast in the kitchen with Sophie had become a habit she had acquired quickly rather than endure the formality of eating on her own in the breakfast room. Today they were interrupted by Carlo, entering to inform them that the helicopter had landed.

Beth walked into the hall and glanced around, her eyes lingering on the family oil paintings that adorned the walls. One day would a painting of her child as an adult hang here? she wondered. Not that she would see it. Once her child was three she would probably never be back here again....

Dante walked in through the door. Her eyes locked with his and then slid away as he crossed the wide expanse of marble floor. Her heart thudded.

'You're looking more lovely than ever, Beth.'

His deep voice played across her nerve-endings.

'How do you feel?'

He cupped her chin in his hand and tilted her head up to his. The familiar male scent of him filled her nostrils. This close he appeared to tower over her, all broad-shouldered and vibrantly male. Shockingly, she had a vivid mental image of his great golden naked body over hers, enclosing her, possessing her. She pressed her trembling thighs together. No way was she telling him how she really felt.

'Fine,' she managed to say, and his mouth descended on hers briefly.

'Sorry I could not be here to show you around. I have missed you,' he said in a deep, husky voice, his dark eyes unreadable as he held her gaze.

Something stirred deep inside Beth and she realised that against all reason she had missed Dante. She opened her mouth to say so, but Sophie burst in with a string of Italian aimed at him that saved her from making a huge mistake. He had obviously only said he missed her for Sophie's benefit.

Five minutes later Beth sat in the helicopter with Dante at the controls. He turned towards her and handed her headphones so they could communicate. Not that she wanted to. The enormity of the day ahead was finally hitting her.

Within an hour they had landed in Rome and were being whisked away from the helicopter in a chauffeured limousine to the hospital. The building looked impressively modern, Beth thought as she entered the luxurious reception area with Dante at her side.

The ultrasound was embarrassing with Dante hovering over her, but as the nurse pointed out the outline of their baby on the screen for an awesome moment they simply stared, then looked at each other and grinned in amazed delight.

Back in the car, Beth looked in wonder at the photo of her child—until she realised the car had stopped.

'My lawyer is expecting us.'

Dante took her arm and helped her out of the car into the offices of his lawyer. In twenty minutes the prenuptial agreement was signed and they were back in the car.

Beth glanced at Dante, a foot away from her in the back seat. He had taken out his smartphone and she presumed he was working. He was certainly efficient, she thought. The speed with which they had seen his lawyer had surprised her. But it should not have done, she realised. Of course he'd wanted absolute proof of the baby before he deigned to give his name to the woman he thought her to be. Thinking about it, she was surprised he had not demanded a DNA test. He didn't trust her any more than she trusted him.

The car drove out of the city and finally through iron gates and up a wide drive, to stop in front of the entrance to a magnificent old building surrounded by perfectly manicured lawns and colourful gardens.

'Is your apartment here?' Beth asked, turning to Dante, sure he was the type to have a super deluxe apartment in the city centre.

'No, I have an apartment on the top floor of the Cannavaro building. But it is more like an extension of my office than a home. I thought you would prefer a hotel so I booked a suite here for two nights.'

Beth was even more amazed, and slightly intimidated as she looked around the elegant sitting room. She glanced at Dante as he handed the porter some money and then turned to walk towards her, and she had the oddest notion that the distinctive, self-assured Dante was not as calm as he appeared.

'You should be comfortable here, Beth. There is an excellent spa and beauty salon, a boutique—everything you could want. And as it is unlucky for the bride to see the groom the night before the wedding, and we need all the luck we can get,' he said dryly. 'I'll leave you to rest and relax. Enjoy the facilities—buy whatever you like. I'll call you tonight to make sure you have everything you need and be back at three tomorrow afternoon to pick you up. The ceremony is at four. Now, order some lunch. I'll see you later.'

Beth watched him walk out through the door, leaving her alone at last. Why did she feel deserted? She dismissed the disturbing thought and prowled around the suite, discovering a bathroom and another room that contained a huge widescreen TV. But there was only one bedroom. Big and beautifully proportioned, with two arched windows and the biggest bed she had ever seen set between them. There was a walk-in closet, and the en-suite bathroom had a double shower, his and hers vanity basins, and a bath wide and deep enough to accommodate two people even as big as Dante.

Ordering a light lunch, she sat down to enjoy the meal. After she had finished eating she thought she would make the most of what was on offer and ordered a spa treatment for eleven the next morning. Then she unpacked and lay down on the bed to rest, the photo of her baby in her hand. This miraculous baby was why she was here, and she would marry the devil himself to keep her child. Her only problem was that she no longer thought of Dante as a devil.... The nightmares of a man in black no longer haunted her. Instead, erotic and sometimes stupidly romantic dreams of a happy-ever-after with Dante had taken their place, and that was what worried her most.

After a stroll around the hotel and gardens she returned to the suite to have a delicious dinner and a surprisingly good night's sleep.

The following afternoon, having been waxed and polished, with her hair styled and her make-up applied to perfection, Beth finally put on the winter-white suit and matching camisole Dante had bought for her in Milan. She slipped her feet into high-heeled shoes, courtesy of the hotel boutique, and walked into the sitting room just as Dante appeared.

'You are ready—good. Let's go and get this over with.'

Beth simply nodded, because the sight of him had taken her breath away. He looked tall and effortlessly elegant in a silver-grey designer suit with a tie shaded in grey, a white silk shirt and the glint of platinum cufflinks. His black hair was brushed back from his brow, his handsome face stern. Lethally attractive, Dante exuded sophistication and innate masculine power—and very soon he would be her husband. The reality terrified her, but if she was brutally honest it also thrilled her, and she had trouble tearing her gaze away.

Half an hour later, intensely conscious of Dante at her side, Beth glanced around the wood-panelled room in the town hall. In her childhood dreams, before real life had caught up with her, she had pictured her wedding as a fairy-tale affair—nothing like this. The suit she wore with its silver trim was as close to bridal as she was ever going to get.

Beth glanced at the celebrant. The man conducted the service in Italian and English, but the ceremony had to be one of the briefest on record.

'You may kiss the bride.'

The words jolted her out of her musings.

She looked up into Dante's eyes as his arms wrapped around her and his lips touched hers, firm and warm and tender. Her hands went to his chest and she felt the beat of his heart beneath her palm as his tongue slipped between her parted lips and found hers. Involuntarily she responded, her body softening against him.

The celebrant cleared his throat and said something to Dante, and his arms tightened around her before reluctantly easing her away.

A camera flashed and Beth blinked.

'Smile, please,' Dante instructed, tucking her arm through his. 'This one is for the baby,' he said, placing a gentle hand on her stomach. 'Every child wants to see a picture of their happy parents on their wedding day— even when the marriage no longer exists.'

'So that is the reason you insisted on buying this suit?' she said, surprised by his forward-thinking.

'Even an autocratic lawyer can have flashes of inspiration sometimes,' he said drolly, and then tugged her arm through his and led her out of the building and into the waiting car.

Back at the hotel, she could not look at him as they ascended the stairs to the first-floor suite. Her panic was mounting with every step as the enormity of what she had done filled her mind. She was married and pregnant and in a few minutes she would be alone with Dante. Her stomach knotted with nerves.

When they reached the suite, Beth's mouth fell open in shock. The elegant suite had been transformed into something incredibly romantic, with dozens of red roses in vases, others in exquisite arrangements, and candles scattered all around. Champagne stood on ice on a silver stand, and next to it was a table exquisitely set for two, with a single red rose in a silver flute as a centrepiece.

'I can't believe this,' Beth said, and Dante reached for her, his hands clasping her waist, drawing her nearer. She felt her body flush with warmth and her pulse quicken.

'Would you believe I'm a romantic at heart? I believe every bride deserves a bridal suite on her wedding night.' He grinned.

Seeing Beth in the hospital had caused a seismic shift in Dante's thinking. For years he had considered her beneath contempt as a drug dealer and the type of immoral woman who would play on her beauty to entrap men for her personal benefit. But when he had seen the scan of their child inside her an emotion he had never experienced before had overwhelmed him. From that moment on he had looked at her in a new way—a different way.

He had sat in the car pretending to work, his mind spinning, and realised she would feel trapped in his apartment, twelve floors up in an elevator. Hurriedly he had booked the hotel. Later he hadn't been able to get out of the suite quickly enough. He'd wanted her so fiercely, but as the mother of his child and his soon-to-be-bride she'd deserved much better than a quick coupling the night before her wedding. He had stopped at

Reception as he left and given strict instructions that she was to be given anything she wanted, and he'd ordered the transformation of the suite for the following afternoon.

Beth looked at Dante, stunned he had bothered. His hand lifted to curl a strand of hair behind her ear, the other slipping behind her to press in the small of her back and hold her close. The brush of his hard male body against her stomach sent heat from low in her pelvis pounding through her veins. Her eyes lifted to the chiselled lips, the sensual mouth. It was impossible to ignore the way her body reacted to his.

But Beth tried. 'No, I wouldn't believe it,' she said, in a last-ditch attempt to deny the fatal attraction Dante held for her.

Her gaze lifted to his dark long-lashed eyes and she felt herself drowning in the glittering depths. She had thought she hated Dante for so many years, but now she wanted him with a hunger and a need for physical contact that she could not control. She raised her hands to his chest....

'I guessed as much,' he murmured, and the teasing brush of his mouth was on hers, making her lips tingle and part. 'But at least give me credit for trying, and allow me to try to prove you wrong.' He chuckled softly and tilted her head to one side. His tongue touched the silken skin below her ear, then trailed kisses down her slender throat.

Beth dragged in a ragged breath and Dante lifted his head, a long finger running along her tremulous lower lip. Dizzy with longing, she instinctively pressed her body closer and felt the jut of his erection against her belly. It was shockingly intimate and incredibly arousing to think she could do this to him, and it made her forget about the past—only the moment and Dante existed.

'Trust me, Beth, today is a new beginning for us, and I want to make it right for you.'

And she did trust him…. Meeting his lips with her own, she signaled her total capitulation.

His mouth explored her with gentle expertise, his tongue curling with hers, teasing, tasting, and she was lost in the wonder of his kiss.

Dante raised his head and had to battle to resist his basic instinct to take her where they stood. He cupped her head in his hands and looked down into her sparkling emerald eyes. The pupils were dilated to black pearls of passion and he stifled a groan.

'Not here, Beth.'

Swinging her up in his arms, he carried her into the bedroom and lowered her gently onto the bed. He had never believed her *once was enough* comment—although ironically it was that one time when he had made her pregnant. But Dante had never suspected Beth was a virgin, and could not help feeling that if he had known he could have done better. Now she was his wife, the mother of his child, and he was determined to give her the wedding night she deserved and would remember with pleasure.

Beth glanced at yet more candles, then stared in awe as Dante stripped off his clothes, his great body gleaming golden in the candlelight. The fine black hair across his chest arrowed down over his washboard stomach to curl at the junction of his thighs, and his powerful erection sent a primordial feminine thrill quivering through her slender frame.

Then he was leaning over her, her clothes were being peeled from her body, and she lay without shame, naked before him, mesmerised by the burning gleam in his eyes as they raked her from head to toe.

'You are exquisite, *mia moglia*,' he rasped, and kissed her forehead, her nose, briefly her lips, and moved lower to her breasts and the soft curve of her stomach, where he lingered, murmuring in Italian.

He raised his head and the intensity in his magnificent dark eyes made her heart squeeze. All her doubts and fears for the future faded away, and she linked her hand around his neck, hungry for his kiss.

Finally his mouth found hers, and she responded intuitively to the searching passion of a kiss that left her breathless and wanting more. Her hands unfurled from his neck to clasp his broad shoulders, while his hands traced slowly and gently over her breasts and stomach, brushing the soft curls as he reached the apex of her thighs. With every silken touch of his fingers Beth's hunger for him grew. Moisture and heat pooled low in her body, which was pulsing with need. His long fingers flicked around her inner thighs, so close to where she ached. His hands swept back up her body, firmer now, cupping her breasts, his thumbs stroking the rosy peaks.

'Slightly larger, I think,' he said huskily, his glittering gaze on her breasts.

His head lowered and his mouth closed over a pouting nipple. She moaned low in her throat. His tongue rolled the rigid tip and his teeth nipped and tugged. The pleasure was almost pain before he licked the throbbing peak and excitement threatened to explode inside her.

Her fingers pressed into his muscular shoulders, nails digging into his flesh. When she could stand no more her hand fisted in his hair to pull his head back, and with a husky groan his mouth closed over hers with the powerful, possessive passion that she hungered for....

His hands, big and strong, caressed her skin and his mouth followed—kissing, tasting, discovering pleasure points she'd never known she had. But Dante knew...

Oh, how he knew...

Beth writhed beneath him, aroused to fever-pitch by his prolonged sensual exploration. His mouth returned to hers, playful, teasing and passionate, while his long fingers continued their delicate exploration of every secret place with an erotic skill that drove her wild....

She was burning up. Her slender hands stroked him and found the thick, hard length of his erection. She knew he was as desperate as she was. With a guttural growl he tore her hand from his body and his mouth found hers again, devouring her. His hands lifted her, and his great body was tense as steel as finally he was where Beth madly, desperately wanted him. He began to probe gently—too gently—and she locked her legs high around his back, her body arching as with supreme control he probed a little deeper, stretching her...

He withdrew.

'Dante!' she cried, desperate for all of him. 'Please!'

With a husky groan and a thrust of his hips he answered her. his hard length filling and holding her. He drew a taut nipple into his mouth and raised his hips and thrust again. Then he paused and suckled its twin, and a starburst of feelings blinded her to everything but Dante. He moved in a fluid, ever increasing rhythm, harder and faster, pulsing inside her until she convulsed around him in a blaze of heat and light, like a star going nova, and she heard his cry of triumph as he followed her, his life force spilling inside her.

'I'm too heavy for you,' Dante rasped some time later, and with a gentle kiss on her love-swollen lips he rolled onto his back and slipped a hand beneath her waist, easing her into the curve of his shoulder.

Beth rested a slender arm across his broad chest. She had thought the first time Dante had made love to her had been incredible, but tonight had surpassed that. She had never felt so complete, so languorous, so perfectly at peace in body and mind in her life.

'How do you feel, Beth? I didn't hurt you, did I?' He stroked the hair back from her brow.

She raised herself up on one elbow and looked down at Dante. His hair was all over the place, his incredible eyes serious, and she let her hand stroke over his chest, her fingers playing with his chest hair. 'No, you didn't hurt me. Though I have to admit...' She paused teasingly, and surprisingly felt his body tense. 'You were right. Once was not enough.'

'Why, you little tease.' He grinned and pulled her head down to his to press his lips against her mouth.

In minutes they were making love again.

Dante took his time to explore her and to show her various ways to please him that surprised and excited both her and Dante! Their senses were on a knife's edge, and when he finally surged up into her with a few pounding thrusts they climaxed together.

Beth lay across Dante's body in the aftermath, totally sated. She had been on top during their lovemaking—something she had never envisaged before—and as her head rested on his chest she found herself too languorous to move. Instead she listened to the heavy pounding of his heart gradually steady.

'Beth?'

Dante said her name and she glanced up at him.

'Sorry to disturb you.' His strong hands clasped her by the waist and he lifted her as if she was as light as a feather and sat up, placing her flat on her back on the bed. 'These damn candles are a fire risk. I can smell burning.'

'So much for romantic gestures,' Beth said, and burst out laughing.

Dante slid out of bed and snuffed out the candles. Beth watched him as he walked to the bathroom. Big and lithe and stunning from the rear, with long legs and firm, tight buttocks—not something she had ever really noticed in a man before, but now she found every inch of Dante fascinating.

They slipped on the robes the hotel had provided and Dante ordered room service. They shared an intimate dinner, and then went back to bed.

The next morning they took a flight to London and Beth fell asleep on the plane....

'Not too bad, hmm...?' Dante said, with a guiding hand on Beth's back as they walked out of his mother's home in Kensington. 'My mother adores you. And when we finally tell her you are pregnant—if she hasn't already guessed—she will worship at your feet. As for Harry— he made his feelings very clear.'

Beth chuckled. 'Yes, he did.' She had been dreading meeting Dante's mother, Teresa—a lovely petite woman, with black hair and brown eyes—and her husband, Harry, but they were a delightful couple and had made her feel completely at ease. Harry was an older version of Tony, and Beth had not been able to help saying so—which had led to her admitting she had lived in the apartment beneath Tony until a few months ago. Dante had added smoothly that that was where Beth and he had met—at Tony's barbecue.

'So *you* are the angel girl who supplied my Tony and Mike with food and all kinds of help!' Teresa had exclaimed, and from then on everything had been plain sailing.

Lunch had been a happy affair, and an eye-opener for Beth as Teresa had regaled her with stories of Dante as a child—much to his embarrassment.

Beth turned now as Teresa and Harry followed them out to say goodbye, with hugs all round and promises to return soon. They were finally about to leave when there was a screech of tyres and Tony arrived.

With a 'Hi, Mum—Dad,' he stopped in front of Beth. 'I don't believe it, Beth! You actually married Dante. What on earth possessed you when you could have had me?' Grinning broadly, he gave her a big hug and a kiss on the cheek. Beth laughed.

'Yes, she did marry me—so you can take your hands off her,' Dante said with a smile that verged on triumphant as he slipped a proprietorial arm around her waist.

'You're a lucky devil, bro, and I'm not surprised you whisked Beth away and married her. I noticed you couldn't take your eyes off her at the barbecue....' Tony said. 'Mind you, I'm not sure you deserve her—'

'That's enough, Tony,' Dante cut in, and the tone of his voice brooked no argument.

'Okay…congratulations. You do make a striking couple. So, where are you going for the honeymoon?'

'Somewhere hot—the Caribbean or the Indian Ocean, as it will be December before I can free up any time. Beth can decide.'

'*I* can decide?' A honeymoon had never entered Beth's head.

'Yes—why not?' Dante gave her a sexy smile. 'I have been all over the place. You can have fun choosing somewhere you would really like to go.'

'Is that wise, Dante?' Tony queried. 'Knowing Beth, it will be a surfers' beach in Hawaii—hardly your scene!' he quipped, then added, 'Trust me, I still shudder at the thought of when she tried to teach Mike and I how to surf.' He grimaced. 'But wherever you go you'd better take good care of her, or you will have me to deal with.'

'I intend to—and thanks.'

'Thank you for that, Tony,' Beth said with a grin. Tony was such a joker, and he enjoyed winding people up, but he was a truly lovable young man.

'Now we really must get going,' Dante commanded, and with final goodbyes all round Beth slid into the passenger seat of the Bentley and they left.

Dante concentrated on negotiating the city traffic, with a frown on his face that had little to do with his driving and everything to do with Beth. Seeing the easy interaction between Beth and his brother, and after spending time with her and getting to know her intimately, he could tell there had never been anything sexual about their relationship. Tony was an irrepressible flirt, like most twenty-three-year-old males, but Beth just laughed and ignored it. And Tony's ready acceptance of their marriage confirmed he had never been serious about her....

Which made Dante question his own actions—not something he was prone to do—in threatening Beth with dire consequences unless she left Tony alone. He now knew a lot of what Beth had told him was the truth, but did it change anything? Her past was inescapable, and he would still have felt duty-bound to tell Tony why she was unsuitable as a wife, conveniently ignoring the fact that *he* had married her.

He cast a sidelong glance at Beth; she looked so relaxed, so beautiful, and she was carrying his child. Yesterday had been their wedding day and last night he had enjoyed the best sex of his life. He only had to look at Beth to want her, and he knew she felt the same. The past was the past and there was no point in dwelling on old mistakes, he told himself.

'You really do like Tony?' he prompted.

'Yes, I do. He is so easygoing, happy and carefree,' she said with a wistful smile. 'It must be nice to be so uncomplicated. What you see with Tony and Mike is what you get, and they make me laugh. I can't remember when I felt young like that—if ever.'

Dante heard the hint of sadness in her tone and could have kicked himself for reminding her of the past; the present and their baby was all that should concern him. 'No wonder they are a carefree pair, with you helping them out all the time.'

'I told you—we're good friends. Though sometimes I think I was more like a house mother to the pair of them.'

Dante shook his head. 'You are far too soft for your own good, Beth.'

* * *

Where Dante was concerned Beth knew she was…. This morning she had awakened in his arms and they had made love again. Bedazzled in the aftermath, she had told him he was a perfect lover. But Dante's response—'I always aim to please, *cara*!'—had struck a discordant note in Beth's mind. Just how many women *had* he pleased? she'd wondered, and it had brought her back to reality.

Dante didn't make love—love never entered his vocabulary. He was a sophisticated man of the world and he must have had sex with dozens of women. The only reason Beth was in his bed was because she was pregnant with his child. She must never think it was anything more than a convenient marriage for the good of her child and herself.

But it was hard when a smiling, tactile Dante was so irresistible as they'd shared breakfast in their hotel suite. He had fed her food from his plate and planted kisses on her mouth between bites. He only had to look at her and she wanted him, and she had to keep reminding herself it wasn't going to last….

She cast Dante a sidelong glance. His focus was on the narrow, twisting country road, but nothing could detract from the sculptured perfection of his profile and her heart skipped a beat.

As if sensing her scrutiny, he slanted a knowing smile her way.

'Not long now.'

Her tummy flipped.

'It's a shame I can only stay one more night. When I get back next weekend we need to discuss more permanent living arrangements.'

Later Beth would wonder if she'd had a premonition that night, when she'd decided to share the main guest bedroom with Dante instead of her own room, the master suite.

CHAPTER TEN

THE LAST DAY of September, and for the past week England had been basking in an Indian summer. The temperature was balmy as Beth walked out of the sea, a smile on her face.

The marriage deal she had struck with Dante that had filled her with such trepidation was turning out to be nothing like what she had feared. The two nights they had shared had been a revelation; he was an incredible lover and generous in every way. Walking up the beach still smiling, Beth realised she actually felt the happiest she had in years.

'On a day like today it makes you glad to be alive,' Beth said, and stopped and grinned down at Janet, who was showing Annie how to build a sandcastle. 'I really enjoyed my swim.' She reached for a towel from her beach bag on the sand and saw her phone flashing. She picked it up and read the text. 'Dante's in a meeting that looks like it's running late. But he will be back here tomorrow evening.' She dropped the phone back in her bag. 'I'll reply later. The waves are rising and I'm going to get my surfboard....'

'No, you won't. A swim is okay, but surfing is definitely out in your condition. And from the black clouds on the horizon it's not going to matter anyway,' Janet said, and rose to her feet. Looking past Beth, she exclaimed, 'Will you look at that? Oh, my God!'

Beth turned to see what Janet meant, and to her horror at the end of the beach she saw a child with a pink plastic ring around her waist, being swept from the shallows by the fast-rising tide.

Beth didn't stop to think—she ran.... A man dashed into the sea and then stopped. Frantic, he yelled that he could not swim, and without hesitation Beth dived into the waves.

What followed was the stuff of nightmares. She managed to reach the child and grab hold of her, but when she tried to turn back the rip tide caught her and they were both swept farther out.

Battling to stay afloat, Beth felt another large wave crash over her, then another, and another. However hard she fought, she could not beat the current, and was being dragged farther out towards the rocky headland. A massive wave submerged them, and for a heart-stopping moment Beth was convinced the end had come. With that came the thought she would never see Dante again....

Suddenly she could breathe again, and with the terrified child's arms locked tightly around her neck Beth twisted to protect her as they were flung against the rocks. She felt a stabbing pain in her back. But the pain in her heart was worse than any gash from the rocks as she realised that against all rhyme and reason she loved Dante.

Clutching the child with the last of her strength, she managed to scramble up onto the rocks. A backward glance told her the tide was coming in fast, and she could not swim back to the shore with the child.

She sat down on a flat rock before her legs gave way completely, cuddling the sobbing child to her chest and breathing great gulps of air into her oxygen-starved lungs in between murmuring words of comfort to the little girl—whose name, she discovered, was Trixie. She had no idea how long she sat there, soothing the child and anxiously watching the water rise. Then she saw the coastguard rescue boat ploughing through the waves and heard someone shouting her name. She rose to her feet, handed Trixie into the outstretched arms of a man in the boat, and almost collapsed with relief— the child was safe.

The rest was a bit of a blur.

She remembered being hauled into the boat, having a blanket wrapped around her and Trixie placed in her arms again. At the harbour an ambulance waited, and Janet had brought her clothes and her bag from the beach. The ambulance crew were insisting on taking them to the hospital.

Later Beth sat in the hospital, with the blanket still around her, waiting to see the doctor. She took her phone out of her bag and read the text Dante had sent her earlier. She texted back that she was fine and that she would see him tomorrow night. She thought of ending with *love*, and didn't quite dare. But Beth knew she loved him without a shadow of a doubt—though she would have preferred to realise it without half drowning in the process.

Perhaps she always had loved Dante? Maybe there *was* such a thing as love at first sight? she mused. All along there had been that deep underlining attraction that had begun in the courtroom when she was only nineteen and too innocent to recognise it, and after the trial it had been easier to hate him. Now she was married to him and carrying his child, and though he didn't love her he wanted her physically. With a child between them she could hope he would grow to love her. The three-year time limit was a minimum, not a maximum....

A young couple with tears in their eyes came up to her and thanked her over and over again for saving their little girl Trixie.

Beth smiled as they walked away, but there was more—much, much more than she had ever expected—until finally she fell into an exhausted sleep.

'Mrs Cannavaro...' Beth opened her eyes and saw a woman in a blue uniform, standing by her bed. She glanced around. The room was white and she was completely disorientated for a moment. Then, as the events of yesterday came flooding back, she closed her eyes again.

'Mrs Cannavaro.'

The nurse repeated her name, and reluctantly she opened her eyes.

'Good news. Your husband will be here soon, and a cup of tea and food is on its way. I need to check your vitals, and then you can have a wash and get dressed,' she told her with a broad smile. 'Dr James will be here to see you soon, and after that you can be discharged. And don't worry—you are very fit and an extremely brave young woman...you will be fine in no time at all.'

The nurse was so unrelentingly cheerful, while avoiding the elephant in the room, that it made Beth want to scream. But she didn't. Stoically, she said, 'Thank you.' And then asked, 'How is Trixie today?'

'Oh, the little girl is fine—thanks to you. She went home with her parents last night.'

'Good,' Beth said, and suffered the nurse's ministrations in silence, reliving the tragic events of yesterday that had put her here. In her mind she blamed herself, though she knew she could never have done anything different. Trixie was safe and that was all that mattered.

But now she was no longer quite so certain.

At nine last night a doctor had told her that the pain that had suddenly doubled her over as she was leaving was the start of a miscarriage. Probably brought on by the tremendous amount of physical energy it had taken to save the little girl. The bruising and the gash on her back had not helped, and it had cost the life of her own baby. By eleven it had all been over, and for the first time since Helen died Beth had broken down and cried until she had no tears left.

Now she felt nothing at all—just totally numb inside.

She nodded and said yes and thank you to the nurse's endless chatter, until finally she was washed and her hair was combed. Wearing the clothes Janet had handed her yesterday, she sat on the edge of the bed and drank a cup of tea. The food was of no interest to her.

Dr James arrived and after checking her over, his eyes full of compassion, he told her how sorry he was and made an appointment for her to see him on Monday to confirm everything was clear. He told her that she was a healthy young woman and he was sure she would have no trouble getting pregnant again when she wanted to, not to worry. It had been an extraordinary set of circumstances that had caused the miscarriage, and it was extremely unlikely to happen again.

Beth smiled and said thank you again, and sat down

on the bed as he turned to leave. She heard the door close behind him. Suddenly the numbness that had protected her bruised mind and body faded away and her shoulders slumped. Her spirit was broken. She could never regret saving Trixie, but it had cost her a soul-destroying price. But then that seemed to be the story of her life, she thought, looking back over the past few years that had led her to this point.

She heard the ring of her cell phone and automatically reached into her bag and answered. It was Janet. She had called at the cottage and the builder was there but Beth wasn't. Janet wanted to know why she was not at home. In a few terse sentences Beth told her, and listened to her compassionate response. She asked if there was anything she could do to help. Beth said nothing except to tell the builders to take the day off. She wanted to be alone for a while, and Dante would be arriving later. She rang off.

Beth did not want to see anyone or talk to anyone. She wanted to close her eyes and forget the last twenty hours had ever happened. But it wasn't to be. She heard the door open again and looked up to see Dante enter the room. His handsome face looked drawn, black stubble shadowed his jaw, and his mouth was a firm straight line. His eyes blazed with some powerful emotion.

Beth saw a chink of light in the darkness of her soul and rose to her feet. She loved him so much. Maybe he would recognise her pain and take it away, fold her in his arms and comfort her. But Dante made no move towards her. He simply stared.

'Beth, how do you feel?'

How many times had he asked her that? she wondered. It seemed to be his favourite question. The chink of light was extinguished. Deep down she had always known it was the baby he was concerned about, not her. And it slowly dawned on her that the emotion she saw in his dark eyes was anger. Why had she expected anything more? He had married her for the baby—nothing else. She had actually fooled herself into thinking that it might have been something more this week and she'd been happy. But not now. The baby was gone and there was no longer any reason for Dante to be here.

The blood turned to ice in her veins; the numbness returning.

'Fine. Can we leave now?'

The fear and the fury Dante had felt since he'd heard the news at midnight eased a little. Beth looked pale and so beautiful, so tragic. He wished he had been here for her. He wanted to take her in his arms...

'I need to get home to feed Binkie.'

'Forget the damn cat!' Dante exclaimed, his fear and anger boiling over. 'I have spoken to the doctor. You have just lost the baby and you are battered and bruised with a slashed back. What on earth possessed you to dive into the sea? You could have died!'

'I am not having this conversation now. If you don't want to drive me home, I'll get a cab.' Beth picked up her bag, refusing to look at him, intent on leaving.

Dante ran a hand though his hair. He had no right to be angry with Beth; she was his wife and she had lost their baby. He had promised to take care of them both and he had spectacularly failed. Worse, he could not control or explain the emotions churning inside him....

He grabbed Beth's arm as she tried to walk past him and spun her into his arms. 'I'm sorry. I didn't mean to upset you.'

Held close against his strong body, Beth felt nothing. It was too little, too late. 'You didn't.' She lifted expressionless eyes to his. 'I have been sitting here thinking of everything that has happened since I first met you and you are right—I am guilty as charged. I did lose your baby.'

'*Dio!* No—I never meant it like that.'

Beth saw the shock in his eyes and didn't care. 'Maybe not, but it is true. What happened yesterday proves the old adage that no good deed goes unpunished, and today I realised it was the story of my life. I offered two boys I thought were friends a lift and ended up in prison. I saved a little girl and lost my own child. I've finally learned it is best not to get involved with anyone. Now, can we leave? I want to get home.'

Dante looked at her pale blank face. The doctor had told him her injuries were not serious—a few scrapes and bruises and a gash that had needed eight stitches. As for the miscarriage—there was to be a minor procedure on Monday and in a week she should be fine. But after losing the baby she might be a little depressed for a while, and he must be patient with her. Dante knew he should not have lost control and shouted at her.

'Yes, of course,' he said softly, and took the bag from her hand. Taking her arm, he left the hospital.

He glanced across at Beth as he drove through the country roads. Her head was back, her eyes closed. Maybe that was best. Dante was not an emotional man, and though he was gutted at the loss of the baby he could not find the words to express how he felt.

Back at the cottage, as soon as Beth walked in the door Binkie was there. Bending, she picked him up in her arms, stroking and murmuring to him as she headed for the kitchen. She put Binkie down and methodically prepared his bowl of chicken. Then she made a pot of coffee—perhaps to prove her baby really was gone.

Dante followed her into the kitchen. 'It is no good ignoring me, Beth. We need to talk about this.'

Beth turned expressionless eyes on him. 'Not now. I am going to have a coffee and then shower and change,' she said in a cool voice.

'I'll join you.'

'For coffee.'

Filling two mugs from the pot, she handed him one. Her emotions were in deep freeze, and she was immune to the brush of Dante's fingers against hers.

She walked back though the house and out onto the terrace. She sat down on one of the captain's chairs, took a sip of coffee and stared out across the sea. The morning sun shimmered on the calm green water and the waves lapped against the fine sand. Her gaze strayed to the headland. As if to mock her, the tide was out and the rocks were barely fifteen feet from the water's edge.

Beth heard a footstep on the terrace but did not turn her head. She took another drink of coffee.

Dante took the chair beside her, his eyes fixed on her delicate profile. 'I honestly didn't mean to upset you any more than you already are, Beth. I know how hard it must be for you. As for me—I have never felt so awful in my life as when I got the call from the hospital and heard what had happened to you. I really wanted our baby. Never doubt that.'

Beth turned her head, her green eyes resting on Dante. She didn't doubt it for a second. She knew he'd wanted the baby. It was her he had never really wanted and had got stuck with.

'It was never meant to be,' she said flatly. 'The baby was conceived for all the wrong reasons. I was stupid, and you wanted me out of your brother's life. If that wasn't bad enough you and I agreed this child was going to be the product of a broken home before it was even born. I don't know what I was thinking of... I must have been out of my mind. But not any more. I've had enough. I love it here. I relocated here to get out of the rat race and this time I am staying.'

'Having got that off your chest, aren't you forgetting something?' Dante prompted. 'You are my wife, and I have some say in your future.'

'Not for much longer. The reason for our marriage is gone. I want nothing from you so we can get divorced straight away. You're a lawyer—I'm sure you can arrange it.' Beth rose to her feet before adding, 'I'm going for a bath.'

Dante watched her walk back inside but didn't follow her. Instead he looked out over the bay, his eyes narrowed as he considered his options. One thing was certain: he was not ready to let Beth go....

The more he got to know her the more he questioned his original assessment of her. She was an amazing woman... He couldn't think of a single female he had ever met who would have leapt into the sea after that child. Most would not risk getting their hair wet, let alone risk their own life, but Beth had.

His angry outburst when he'd first seen her hadn't been because she had lost the baby but because he had feared for her life....

Rising to his feet, he strolled back into the house.

* * *

With the dressing on her back in mind, Beth had had a bath in about nine inches of water. Stepping out, she took a towel and carefully dried her aching body. She found an old blue tracksuit in one of the drawers. It had loose pants, so would not press against the cut on her back. Then, barefoot, she walked into the bedroom, slid open the glass door to the balcony and stepped outside. She sank down on a lounger, safe in her haven, and closed her eyes.

'Beth?'

Reluctantly she opened her eyes at the sound of her name, and saw Dante walking out of her bedroom on to the balcony, carrying a tray.

She sat up abruptly. 'What are you doing here? This is my room.'

'Looking for you. I was under the impression the room you and I shared last Sunday was the master bed-room, but I see I was wrong. This is much larger,' he said, his dark eyes resting on her.

Beth didn't need reminding of that day. 'If you've brought me food you can take it away. I'm not hungry and I want to be alone.'

He put the tray down across her knees. 'What you want and what you need are entirely different,' he said and, pulling up a lounger, sat down.

'Now, eat. I am going to sit here until you do.'

Beth looked at the plate of open sandwiches—ham, cheese, egg, tomatoes, salami and prawns, plus a token couple of lettuce leaves. 'You must have raided the fridge for this lot.'

'I did—to tempt your tastebuds. In the last twenty-four hours you have been tested to the limit physically and emotionally with the loss of the baby. You need to build up your strength again.'

She picked up an egg sandwich and realised she had not eaten since lunch yesterday. She took a bite and found she could finish it. 'There's no need for you to stay. I *am* eating.'

She glanced up into the black brooding intensity of Dante's dark eyes without a flicker of emotion in her own.

'I am staying. Not just to see you eat, but for as long as it takes to make sure you are fully recovered.'

Spoken like the despot he was, Beth thought. But it didn't bother her. She was immune to him now. And from what she knew of Dante he was not cut out for the quiet life of Faith Cove. He'd be bored out of his mind in a couple of days and would go back to his high-flying life. She'd never see him again.

'Please yourself. You usually do. As long as you understand you are not sharing my room.' He didn't argue and she wasn't surprised. With no sex available, why would he?

By Monday morning, when he insisted on going to the hospital with her, Beth was not quite so sure he would leave. He was a good house guest. He cooked—though not very well—he made his bed in his own room, and he had clothes delivered and his laundry collected by a concierge service. Yes, he had a tendency to wrap an arm around her or drop a kiss on her brow, but it had no effect on her.

Over dinner on Tuesday night Beth had a rude awakening.

Dante was not the most patient of men, and being

blanked by Beth for four days was getting to him. When he touched her she was like a block of ice. If he told her to eat, she did. If he suggested a walk, she agreed. To-night he had cooked spaghetti, one of the few dishes he could make well, and she had sat down like an obedient child. He'd had enough. He wanted the feisty Beth back.

Dante watched her full lips part as she forked food into her mouth and felt the familiar tug of desire. She wore no make-up, her glorious hair was swept severely back from her face—she looked beautiful, but remote.

'My mother called me today and she sends you her love. She hopes to see us soon. As she missed our wed-ding, she wants to arrange a post-wedding party for family and friends. I agreed. I think a party will do you good. I have to be in New York next week, probably for three or four weeks, so I suggested mid-November.'

Beth couldn't believe her ears. 'A party? No way! We are getting a divorce, remember?'

'I recall you mentioned divorce, but you were ill so I said nothing.'

The way Dante was looking at her suddenly made Beth feel threatened. He was big and golden, and the dark glitter in his eyes, the slightly predatory curl of his mouth, contained a message she did not want to recog-nize. She knew she had to tread carefully.

'But I thought you'd agreed when you didn't say any-thing against it?'

'We had just got back from the hospital. I did not want to upset you and I certainly wasn't going to argue with you. You *did* read the prenuptial agreement?'

'Yes, of course.' Beth didn't get the connection.

'Then you must know you have not fulfilled your part of the deal.'

'What do you mean?' From just *feeling* threatened Beth knew she was being threatened, and she received an answer that astounded her.

'It states quite clearly that three years after the birth of our first child I will agree to give you a divorce if you so desire. As sadly we don't have a child yet, I don't have to give you anything—certainly not a divorce unless I want to, and right now I don't want to.'

'Are you telling me I have to get pregnant again?' Beth exclaimed.

'Hell, no. I am not that much of an ogre. Though it is something we could consider in the future.'

Beth stood up, her green eyes flashing. 'You and I don't have a future together. We never did. I'm going to bed.'

Dante had seen the angry sparkle in her eyes and knew he was getting through to her. 'I'll walk you to your room.'

Where had she heard that before?

Beth remembered and felt a slight flutter in her tummy—which wasn't helped by Dante's strong arm curving around her waist. The numbness that had protected her was fading fast, but she didn't want to be aware of him again, and said, 'You are hurting my back.' She spun out of his arm and out through the door.

Dante was going to follow her, but hesitated. She had suffered a traumatic shock with the miscarriage. He could wait until tomorrow. Because he had sensed when he held her the ice had broken. He was winning her over. He simply had to persevere a little longer.

Beth undressed and got into bed, but she couldn't sleep. She heard Dante walk upstairs and the door of his room open and close. She heaved a sigh of relief tinged with regret for what might have been if she had not lost her baby....

By the time Beth crawled into bed on Thursday night she could no longer pretend she was immune to Dante. On Wednesday she had tried to avoid him by working in her study. But as the study looked out over the back garden she had caught sight of Dante, stripped to the waist, helping the builders. She had not been able to tear her gaze away from him, and suddenly the unseasonably warm weather had felt even hotter. And this morning when he'd slipped his arm around her waist she had trembled. She had blamed it on the cut on her back.

'Back still sore, Beth? I thought the stitches dissolved in seven days,' Dante had drawled mockingly. He'd known perfectly well she was faking it, and exactly how he affected her....

This evening had been the final straw. He had insisted on taking her to the pub for a meal, saying she needed to get out. She had watched him, looking devastatingly attractive in blue jeans and a grey sweater, laughing and talking with easy charm with the other customers, thinking of how patient he was being with her when she had expected him to be long gone. She knew she was in big trouble. She loved him and it terrified her.

Beth had told herself so often that she hated him, but her heart told her something else. He said he didn't want a divorce and would like another child. If she actually was the type of woman he thought she was it would be easy to stay married to him—handsome, rich and good at sex. She stirred restlessly in the bed. But she wasn't that type of woman.

She loved him, and staying married to him would

destroy her. He was convinced she was guilty of a hei-
nous crime and that would never change. He wanted her
and he felt affection for her—he'd proved that by staying and caring for her this week—but there could never
be any equality in their relationship. She would always
be the guilty party, inferior in his mind and not really
to be trusted, and she could not live with that. Without
trust there was nothing. She had fought long and hard
to be a successful woman in her own right and she was
not prepared to be an appendage to Dante's life.

When Beth finally fell asleep her decision was made.

CHAPTER ELEVEN

BETH OPENED HER EYES and glanced sleepily at her alarm clock. Nine o'clock. She blinked and studied the clock again. She must have slept through the seven o'clock alarm.

She stretched luxuriously beneath the covers and then pushed them back so she could get up. When the door opened and Dante walked in her first instinct was to dive back under the covers, but that would be childish, so she settled for sitting up and pulling her nightshirt down her legs.

'Good morning, Beth. Did you sleep well?'

'Yes, thank you. Did you?'

Their eyes met briefly. 'Not as well as I would have done with you,' he said.

He was wearing black jeans and a sweater and he was smiling down at her. Suddenly she was filled with the most intense sensual message, and though outwardly motionless she quivered inside.

'I was about to get up,' she said hastily.

'So I see.' He sat down on the side of the bed and wrapped his hand around her wrist. 'But I need to talk to you first. The manager of my New York office called me when we got back last night in something of a panic.

I have to be at an emergency meeting there tomorrow. It's all going to be a bit of a rush. Our flight is booked for five this afternoon from Heathrow, so we will have to leave soon.'

'We?' Beth interjected. 'Why? This has nothing to do with me.'

Suddenly he lifted her wrist and wrapped his arm around her to draw her close. His mouth covered hers, his tongue stroking and delving into the sensitive interior. All her logic of last night was forgotten as she was swept up to the dizzy heights of passion by his kiss.

'*That* is why,' Dante rasped, looking into her eyes. 'I want you with me.'

Beth was almost convinced by the taste of him on her lips and the tight knot of desire in her stomach—until he added, 'I spoke to the builder when he arrived this morning and you don't have to be here. If he needs to get in the house he can get the keys from Janet or her father. And Janet has agreed to take the cat for the three or four weeks we will be away. All you need to do is pack a few things.'

Beth was stunned. From dizzy heights back to earth in one moment. Dante really had thought of everything—except asking her first. She'd been right. She was just an appendage to his life.

Withdrawing her hand from his shoulder, she eased away from him. 'Just one query.' She raised a delicate eyebrow. 'Do you want me with you for sex, or because you are madly in love with me?' she asked, putting him on the spot. She noted the hint of colour that accentuated his high cheekbones and saw the answer in his eyes.

'I want you with me because you're my wife.'

Clever sidestep, worthy of a good lawyer, Beth
thought, and was amazed at how quickly passion could
fade. Sliding her legs over to the opposite side of the
bed, she stood up and turned to look at him. He was
the most handsome man she had ever seen, and she
loved him so much. But a one-sided love was a recipe
for disaster, and she had had enough of those in her
life already.

'I want to stay here and get a divorce. So I guess we
will have to agree to differ,' she said with a noncha-
lance she didn't feel.

Dante rose to his feet, seething with anger and frustration. If he had said he loved her they would be in
that bed now, but he refused to be manipulated by any
woman. He had spent a week waiting on her when he
should have been working—something he had never
done for any other woman. In fact he didn't know what
the hell he was waiting for, wasting his time. He glanced
furiously around. Beth could stay in this place she loved
so much. He didn't need her in his life, compromising
his work. She could have her damned divorce.

'No. You can have a divorce—and a word of advice.
I know your cellmate died in your arms in this room.
It's time you got the place decorated instead of hanging
on to your less-than-salubrious past like a safety blanket, or you will never move on in life.'

And with that parting shot he stormed out.

Beth watched him go. His last unemotional parting
comment had cut deep but proved what she'd known all
along. How could she still love him? She was glad he
was gone. It was what she wanted, she told herself. So
why did she feel like crying? She glanced around the
room, seeing it through Dante's eyes. The décor was

faded. She ran her hand along the bureau, remembering the first time she had made love with Dante in this room—because for her it *had* always been love. Dante was right. It was time she moved on instead of clinging to the past. Just not with him....

December, and Dante was back in London, seated next to Martin Thomas, an acquaintance from his university days, at the Law Society's annual dinner. He was regretting that he had come, but he regretted a lot lately. Especially walking out on Beth. Why hadn't he just told her he loved her? If the last two months without her had taught him anything it was that he couldn't live without her—and if that wasn't love he didn't know what was.

'You know old Bewick, don't you, Dante?' Martin asked. Not waiting for a response, he continued, 'You have to feel sorry for him. He doted on that son of his—Timothy. It must have come as one hell of a shock to him to hear he was arrested for drug smuggling.'

'What? His son? Are you sure?' Dante asked, frowning.

'No doubt about it. Baby Face Bewick is one of the biggest suppliers of drugs in the country. The drug squad had his operation under surveillance for a year, and now they've arrested him and his sidekick, Hudson, and recovered drugs worth over two million. The two of them were refused bail and are in jail awaiting trial. I'm prosecuting the case and it is watertight—plus Hudson is singing like a canary. Bewick started dealing drugs while at public school, apparently. Hudson helped him and they continued at university. Actually they were nearly caught in the first term, but they fitted up some teenage girl—Jane someone—and got away with it. Hudson probably wishes he hadn't now. Juvenile detention would have been much easier than where he is going.'

Dante had heard enough. Abruptly he got to his feet and walked out.

The next morning he called a friend at Scotland Yard and confirmed that Jane Mason was the girl who had been set up and given three years in jail. She was probably in line for some hefty compensation....

Twelve days to Christmas, and after a day shopping with Janet and Annie Beth waved them off and unpacked her purchases—gifts, decorations, food, stuff for the apartment that was now finished. Beth was feeling good.

Later that night, after spending ages looping a new string of one hundred Christmas lights around the tree, she decided the baubles could wait till tomorrow. Beth took a shower, then curled up on the sofa wearing an oversized T-shirt and a white fleece robe. Binkie curled against her leg, purring like a train. A log fire burned in the open grate, and she reached to stroke Binkie's back just as the doorbell rang—and rang again. She glanced at the mantel clock—eight-thirty.

Who could it be? she wondered. Probably church carol singers, she thought as she walked down the hall and opened the door. She pulled her robe tighter around her as a blast of cold air hit her and looked up with a welcoming smile—before her mouth fell open. Not carol singers. Dante... Her heart lurched in her breast.

Dante saw Beth in the doorway, covered in a long white robe and smiling, her green eyes sparkling bright and clear. The hall light behind her picked up the sheen of her red hair and formed a halo around her head. She looked like an angel, and the guilt and despair he felt almost overwhelmed him.

'What are you doing here?' Beth asked when she had recovered her breath.

'I need to see you. It's important, Beth. Please invite me in. This won't take long.'

She didn't want to invite him in, but it was freezing cold. 'All right.' She stood back and waved him inside, closing the door behind him, then turned to see him watching her.

In the light she was shocked by how gaunt he looked. His high cheekbones were sharper, his mouth a grim line, his eyes were deeper in their sockets, and she saw pain in the dark depths. But for her he was still the most beautiful man she had ever seen—and she had thought she was getting over him....

'Come and sit down.' She walked into the room where the fire burnt brightly. 'Let me take your coat.' He was wearing a heavy black overcoat, and after slipping it off he handed it to her. 'Would you like a hot drink?' His cream sweater hung loosely on his tall frame, the denim jeans were not such a close fit, and she wondered what had happened to him. He looked ill.

He straightened his shoulders. 'No, thank you.' Binkie leapt off the sofa and padded over to rub against Dante's leg. 'Hi, Binkie,' he said, and the glimmer of a smile twisted his stern mouth.

Traitorous cat, Beth thought. But in the week when Dante had stayed with her he had made friends with Binkie.

She folded his coat and laid it over the back of an armchair. Now she was over the shock of seeing him the disturbingly familiar scent of his aftershave, his hair, his skin was reaching her, reminding her of intimate moments she had fought hard to forget. Her breasts swelled. A quiver of sensation flowed through her body.

Beth tensed and walked past him to curl up on the sofa again. 'Why are you here?' she asked. She had never heard from him since he had walked out, and had been expecting divorce papers. 'To deliver the divorce papers personally?' she queried. She could think of no other reason.

'No. Timothy Bewick.'

Beth sat up straight at that, and looked Dante squarely in the eyes. 'This is my home, and I will not have that name mentioned in it,' she said firmly. 'I'd like you to leave.'

'I will. But first I want to apologise—though I know no apology can begin to excuse what I did to you. That is why I am here.' He looked uncomfortable and uncertain, and Beth was intrigued. 'If you will just hear me out, Beth, and then you will probably throw me out— which is no more than I deserve.'

'What are you apologising for?' Beth was totally mystified.

Dante straightened his shoulders, bracing himself to continue. 'Last night I found out that Baby Face Bewick, as he is now known, is one of the biggest suppliers of drugs in this country and is currently in jail with Hudson, awaiting trial. Hudson has admitted they once set up a girl—you—Jane Mason—to take the fall for them as teenagers.'

Beth shrugged. 'So? I've always known I'm innocent, and it doesn't matter now. Life has moved on.'

'It matters to me,' Dante said in a driven tone, his

glittering dark eyes raw with pain and regret. 'I can barely live with myself, knowing what I did to you. I put you in prison—stole eighteen months of your life. When I think what you must have suffered it tears me up inside. Your claustrophobia—and worse, I'm sure— is all down to me. I can't believe I was so arrogant, so blind as to fall for the lies.'

'Don't beat yourself up about it. Nobody's infallible—not even you. As you said yourself, any decent lawyer would have got the same result.' Now he knew the truth Beth felt vindicated, and pleased in a way, but seeing the cool, arrogant Dante humbled was not as satisfying as she'd used to imagine it would be.

'How can you be so calm, Beth? I ruined your life,' he said vehemently.

'Because I have lived with the knowledge for years and there is no point in letting bitterness take over. That way you only destroy yourself.'

'*Dio*, Beth.' He moved and sat down beside her. 'When I think of how I behaved when I met you again… I threatened you, said hateful things. I am sorry from the bottom of my heart, though I know no apology can ever make up for the way I treated you. But I had to come and see you—tell you. Beth, you deserve that much and so much more. The irony of it is I was regretting going to that dinner—I was regretting not telling you I love you—and then I heard about Bewick.'

He grabbed her hands in his and squeezed them so hard she winced, but he seemed not to notice. Beth was reeling in shock from his 'I love you'. Her heart was racing, and suddenly she was aware of the warmth of his breath on her face as he studied her with incredible intensity.

'I understand why you said you hated me, Beth, and I don't blame you. I hate myself. I'm amazed you could even bear to speak to me.' The raw emotion in his tone was unmistakable. 'I'd give everything I own—my life—to give you back the time that was stolen from you.'

His grip tightened on her hands as he gazed at her with those incredible dark eyes, and all of a sudden it was as if the world was standing still…waiting. Beth was intensely aware of the slow pulse of her blood flowing though her veins, every breath she drew, and the silence lengthened. She had the oddest notion that Dante was afraid.

'I don't expect you to forgive me. And I know I have no right to ask this—not after what I have done. But I love you so much. If you could find it in your heart to give me another chance… I'm not asking you to love me, Beth, just to let me back in your life—let me try to make amends. Please.'

Beth's heart overflowed. Dante sounded so vulnerable, and the 'please' brought moisture to her eyes. He had said he loved her not once, but twice, and she wanted to believe him. So she did, and it felt as if all her Christmases had come at once.

'Yes,' she said, expecting to be swept into his arms

Instead Dante lifted her hand and kissed her palm almost reverently. 'Thank you, *cara*.' His mouth brushed hers gently. 'I know I don't deserve you, but I do love you, and I swear I will spend the rest of my life making it up to you,' Dante murmured, his tongue seeking entry to her mouth.

Warmed by his words, she opened to him. Her heartbeat quickened and she wrapped her arms around him and put her heart and soul into the kiss.

He eased her robe off her shoulders and she slipped her arms free to wrap them around his neck. She felt his hands skim down to her thighs, felt the slide of her T-shirt up to her hips and lifted herself to help him slip it over her head. She watched as he stood up and stripped off his clothes, and there, with the log fire burning and the fairy lights glittering, they lay on the long sofa kissing, caressing lovingly.

She trembled at the heated stroke of his hands over her shoulders, her breasts, down to her stomach and thighs, his long fingers running gently over her silken skin as if worshipping her body. Beth encouraged him with muted sighs, her delicate hands sliding down his great torso to settle on his taut buttocks.

They made love slowly, and Dante tasted and touched— as did Beth.

Finally their senses were at breaking point and their bodies joined in frantic need, pulsing, plunging, senses on fire as the climax hit and release shuddered through them both.

Beth lay breathless, her body quivering, and Dante tucked her up against him and stroked her hair.

'I can't believe this has happened. I came here to-night in the pit of despair, not really expecting you to let me in. You have such a generous heart. You are beautiful inside and out. I will spend the rest of my life and beyond loving you.'

Beth looked up into his incredible eyes. Love was plain to see in the gleaming depths. 'And I love you. I think I always did. I saw you in court and thought you were my knight in shining armour—my saviour. It has taken a long time, but now I *know* you are.'

He swept her up in his arms and carried her up to the bedroom they had last shared, where they made sweet love all over again.

Dante loved her in every way, Beth thought happily, and yawned widely. Cuddled against his big body, she slept.

Dante watched her sleeping and could not believe his luck. She had forgiven him and taken him back—this beautiful, brave, wonderful woman he would love till the day he died and beyond. He pressed a gentle kiss on her cheek. Then he realised he had made the same mistake again and forgotten protection. He considered waking Beth, but decided against it. She would find out soon enough.

He folded her closer in his arms and fell asleep.

Eleven months later a huge party was held at the Cannavaro estate, for all the family and friends of Dante and Beth, to celebrate their wedding—admittedly a little late—and also the christening of Francesco Cannavaro, their new son and heir. Much to his grandmother's delight—and Sophie's—they finally got to wear their wedding hats.

* * * * *

Mills & Boon® Hardback
April 2013

ROMANCE

Master of her Virtue	Miranda Lee
The Cost of her Innocence	Jacqueline Baird
A Taste of the Forbidden	Carole Mortimer
Count Valieri's Prisoner	Sara Craven
The Merciless Travis Wilde	Sandra Marton
A Game with One Winner	Lynn Raye Harris
Heir to a Desert Legacy	Maisey Yates
The Sinful Art of Revenge	Maya Blake
Marriage in Name Only?	Anne Oliver
Waking Up Married	Mira Lyn Kelly
Sparks Fly with the Billionaire	Marion Lennox
A Daddy for Her Sons	Raye Morgan
Along Came Twins…	Rebecca Winters
An Accidental Family	Ami Weaver
A Date with a Bollywood Star	Riya Lakhani
The Proposal Plan	Charlotte Phillips
Their Most Forbidden Fling	Melanie Milburne
The Last Doctor She Should Ever Date	Louisa George

MEDICAL

NYC Angels: Unmasking Dr Serious	Laura Iding
NYC Angels: The Wallflower's Secret	Susan Carlisle
Cinderella of Harley Street	Anne Fraser
You, Me and a Family	Sue MacKay

Mills & Boon® Large Print
April 2013

ROMANCE

A Ring to Secure His Heir	Lynne Graham
What His Money Can't Hide	Maggie Cox
Woman in a Sheikh's World	Sarah Morgan
At Dante's Service	Chantelle Shaw
The English Lord's Secret Son	Margaret Way
The Secret That Changed Everything	Lucy Gordon
The Cattleman's Special Delivery	Barbara Hannay
Her Man in Manhattan	Trish Wylie
At His Majesty's Request	Maisey Yates
Breaking the Greek's Rules	Anne McAllister
The Ruthless Caleb Wilde	Sandra Marton

HISTORICAL

Some Like It Wicked	Carole Mortimer
Born to Scandal	Diane Gaston
Beneath the Major's Scars	Sarah Mallory
Warriors in Winter	Michelle Willingham
A Stranger's Touch	Anne Herries

MEDICAL

A Socialite's Christmas Wish	Lucy Clark
Redeeming Dr Riccardi	Leah Martyn
The Family Who Made Him Whole	Jennifer Taylor
The Doctor Meets Her Match	Annie Claydon
The Doctor's Lost-and-Found Heart	Dianne Drake
The Man Who Wouldn't Marry	Tina Beckett

Mills & Boon® Hardback

May 2013

ROMANCE

A Rich Man's Whim	Lynne Graham
A Price Worth Paying?	Trish Morey
A Touch of Notoriety	Carole Mortimer
The Secret Casella Baby	Cathy Williams
Maid for Montero	Kim Lawrence
Captive in his Castle	Chantelle Shaw
Heir to a Dark Inheritance	Maisey Yates
A Legacy of Secrets	Carol Marinelli
Her Deal with the Devil	Nicola Marsh
One More Sleepless Night	Lucy King
A Father for Her Triplets	Susan Meier
The Matchmaker's Happy Ending	Shirley Jump
Second Chance with the Rebel	Cara Colter
First Comes Baby...	Michelle Douglas
Anything but Vanilla...	Liz Fielding
It was Only a Kiss	Joss Wood
Return of the Rebel Doctor	Joanna Neil
One Baby Step at a Time	Meredith Webber

MEDICAL

NYC Angels: Flirting with Danger	Tina Beckett
NYC Angels: Tempting Nurse Scarlet	Wendy S. Marcus
One Life Changing Moment	Lucy Clark
P.S. You're a Daddy!	Dianne Drake

0413 GEN STD HB

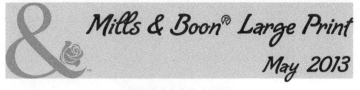

Mills & Boon® Large Print
May 2013

ROMANCE

Beholden to the Throne	Carol Marinelli
The Petrelli Heir	Kim Lawrence
Her Little White Lie	Maisey Yates
Her Shameful Secret	Susanna Carr
The Incorrigible Playboy	Emma Darcy
No Longer Forbidden?	Dani Collins
The Enigmatic Greek	Catherine George
The Heir's Proposal	Raye Morgan
The Soldier's Sweetheart	Soraya Lane
The Billionaire's Fair Lady	Barbara Wallace
A Bride for the Maverick Millionaire	Marion Lennox

HISTORICAL

Some Like to Shock	Carole Mortimer
Forbidden Jewel of India	Louise Allen
The Caged Countess	Joanna Fulford
Captive of the Border Lord	Blythe Gifford
Behind the Rake's Wicked Wager	Sarah Mallory

MEDICAL

Maybe This Christmas...?	Alison Roberts
A Doctor, A Fling & A Wedding Ring	Fiona McArthur
Dr Chandler's Sleeping Beauty	Melanie Milburne
Her Christmas Eve Diamond	Scarlet Wilson
Newborn Baby For Christmas	Fiona Lowe
The War Hero's Locked-Away Heart	Louisa George